The LEGEND OF

YUCK-MAN

The LEGEND OF
YUCK-MAN

Smarak Swain

Srishti
PUBLISHERS & DISTRIBUTORS

SRISHTI PUBLISHERS & DISTRIBUTORS
Registered Office: N-16, C.R. Park
New Delhi – 110 019
Corporate Office: 212A, Peacock Lane
Shahpur Jat, New Delhi – 110 049
editorial@srishtipublishers.com

First published by
Srishti Publishers & Distributors in 2015

10 9 8 7 6 5 4 3 2 1

This is a work of fiction. The characters, places, organisations and events described in this book are either a work of the author's imagination or have been used fictitiously. Any resemblance to people - living or dead - and places is purely co-incidental.

The author asserts the moral right to be identified as the author of this work.

Prologue

A few years back there were a series of attacks by a mysterious offender on a major Indian city. The offender's acts were blatant and outrageous. He killed at random, committed sexual crimes, and kidnapped young women. Most attacks took place in crowded public places such as hotels, discotheques, and shopping malls. Yet this person remains a mystery. All that the eyewitnesses could say was – he was ugly, smelt repugnant, and was generally loathsome. They also swore that this individual had superhuman powers.

He was the talk of the town after each of his bold attacks. Some of his most audacious attacks took place in broad daylight. Fear ruled the hearts of people. No one had imagined that a city of such size, wealth and power could ever be held under siege by just one person. But then, you can correct me; he was not a person, he was a monster.

His attacks have stopped. No one knows where Yuckman – as this filthy monster was nicknamed – came from. No one knows what happened to him. No one cares anymore. People have forgotten him.

That does not make the story of Yuckman any less extraordinary. This is the true, untold biography of Yuckman.

Yuckman Origins

The story of Yuckman faded into oblivion in public imagination as fast as it had fired. The only place he finds mention now is in bonfire stories of urban legends – in the same breath and fascination as milk – drinking Ganesha idols, the stoneman and the monkeyman. No wonder the story remains arbitrary and absurd. More myth and trifling truth. Was he a sorcerer? Was he a demon? What was his political stand? What were his objectives? Is he still around?

No one asks his name, liberally assuming that his type of creatures do not have one. As if he popped out of a sacrificial fire after some saffron-clad Himalayan sages managed to please the fire god. His name was Sibu. Sibu of the Tikna tribe from the impoverished Koraput district of Odisha. His ancestral village I cannot name for it does not exist anymore. In fact, it had ceased existing long before he was born.

Sibu's ancestral village was located on a hill in a densely forested stretch of the Eastern Ghats. The village had remained secluded from human civilisation for ages. It was only in the 1960s that a team of geologists discovered the village. They had gone deep into the Koraput jungle on an iron ore exploration project. Later, many anthropologists and social workers established contact with the village and nearby villages, the primordial habitat of the Tikna tribe. One anthropologist from Belgium went on to publish a monograph on the culture and traditions of Tikna tribe.

Sibu's ancestors' mistake was that they had settled on a hill that had ample deposits of high grade iron ore. The mine was leased out to a company by the state government (the company also managed to get a certificate that the hill is barren and mining activity would not have significant environmental impact).

One fine day, a handful of policemen went to the village and vacated it. The company was set to start mining in the village, and they thought this was a good strategy. Companies were getting frustrated by the growing number of mass movements against displacement. Such movements would stall operations for years. The natives would not take tempting offers having been misled and brain-washed by political parties and worse, the leftists. So in this case, the police dropped by one fine day along with company agents and evicted the village. Men, women, children, chickens, goats, and utensils were loaded in trucks and transported to a new housing complex on the outskirts of Jeypore town. The village pradhan had been taken into confidence by the company agents. The pradhan, using his wise judgment, preferred not to explain the exact nature of the eviction and presented it as a picnic outing.

As reality dawned in ensuing days, there were some objections. Some elders reproached the pradhan for not consulting them. But what was done was done. That village was gone, and this was the new one. Was this not beautiful, the pradhan reasoned? He also disclosed that the company had given each family five lakh rupees in compensation and a cemented house in this complex. That eased the atmosphere. Five lakhs was a big amount. The villagers realised how the wise pradhan had made them all so rich so suddenly. The villagers had a good party that night. In addition to the locally distilled *handia* and *kusna,* foreign liquor also flowed.

Foreign liquor flowed for days as they got a touch of modern life. Men no longer had to do traditional farming and collect firewood (there was an electricity connection in the new village and the company had generously provided gas subscriptions). They did not know the ways of townsfolk or what kind of jobs could be taken up in the town. Their worldview had always been limited by the ways of their village. Neither could they search for a new job, nor was there any place in the town they could work in. Out of work, they had a lot of idle time to party.

After a while, the money dried out, but the flow of foreign liquor did not stop. The local liquor trader was kind enough to let the party continue on credit. After a few more days, the liquor trader arrived with a long list of monies they owed him. He explained how much he suffered, how he ran his business at extremely low liquidity, just because he honoured his friendship with the tribe. The villagers unanimously decided that it was unfair of them to party every day while their friend was suffering at their cost. There had to be a way out. The liquor trader proposed that he could put the houses on mortgage and the flow of liquor would continue uninterrupted. This seemed to be a good idea. A few elders even joked that they had outsmarted the liquor trader: they continued to live in their houses and continued drinking drink his liquor, and the poor fellow thought his dues had been paid. They just had to put their thumb impressions on a few papers and the party continued.

A few weeks later, a builder came to the area. He claimed that all houses in the area belonged to him. How could that be? The company had given *them* the land and the houses. The builder showed them some papers and stated that he had purchased the houses from the liquor trader as per law of the land.

The residents opposed this move vehemently, reasoning that the company be called as witness. If they gave up the houses, they'd need their land back in the village. The local police station was informed that these tribals were holding on to the next day, the builder's property illegally. The police came and threatened the illiterate fools to leave before sunrise. At sunrise the next day, the builder's goons came and loaded the children, chickens, goats and utensils on a truck. Mothers and fathers had no choice but to hop on. There were minor skirmishes but the wise elders stopped the unruly youth from resorting to violence.

The new settlement colony was a small patch of land some villagers had stumbled upon on the Koraput-Jeypore highway. The village had been segregated. The pradhan had made wise financial decisions and was doing well. He had also managed to get his son employed in the company. Fearing that the villagers may turn to him for help, he moved to another part of Jeypore town. Certain families that had spent too lavishly were in heavy debt. Their debt was too high for the liquor trader to pardon them. They were packed up and sent cross-border to Andhra Pradesh to work in brick-kilns till they repaid the debt with interest. Of what was left of the village, one family was that of Anta Oraon.

Anta Oraon had sold his wife Mali to Saanta Oraon when they were still in the company resettlement colony. He was drunk and needed money for a gambling game and sold off his wife. Later when he came to his senses, he promised Saanta Oraon that he would return the money by taking a loan from the liquor trader, from whom everyone took loans. But Saanta Oraon rejected the offer as he had had his eye on Mali for a long time.

In their teen years Saanta and Mali had spent many romantic evenings together. They made a lovely couple and everyone thought that Saanta would marry Mali. However, Saanta could not muster the bride price demanded by Mali's father, who then gave her away to Anta. Ages and three children later, Saanta Oraon was still seething in his desire for Mali.

The matter was referred to the village elders. The elders discussed precedence and instances of such a case and gave the considered opinion that Mali would be wife of both Anta Oraon and Saanta Oraon. In the new hamlet, Mali was mistress of two huts. Having lost both men to liquor, she was now the only bread-winner for both families. Devoid of land and forest produce, she tried to get the job of a maid. Previously in their village, a Tikna tribe girl would kill herself rather than work as a maid. But times were changing, and she had many hungry mouths to feed. She got a good offer in the house of the local revenue inspector (RI).

Koraput was 'punishment posting' for the said RI. For that matter any RI. His wife and kids had not come along with him. (The kids would not get good education here). He needed a full time maid who would cook for him and be his homemaker. Mali easily fitted the role. She was clean, meticulous, caring, and cooked well.

The RI grew fond of her, but more so of her body. He was amazed by her curves. Mali was dark complexioned and had smooth skin. Tribal women labour hard and hence the three childbirths did not show on her. If at all, they had contributed to increasing the tank capacity of her breasts. The RI drew up a plan and made his move. Mali was in the kitchen when he came from behind and grabbed her. He groped her bosom and planted kisses all over her. Mali tried to resist a little, but not much. The wife of two and mother of three had not been given any indulgences lately. She had wondered often how it would feel to sleep on the cosy bed she made for the RI. Besides, there was the awe of a babu falling for her. They had a short love life which they both enjoyed and Mali cherished. Not long after, the rumours started spreading and the babu had to dispose her with a generous tip.

It was under the above circumstances that Sibu was born to Mali. Not even Mali was sure who the father was. When Anta would get drunk and violent, he would come, beat her up and jump onto her. Saanta was aware that he had equal rights over her and would keep a tab of how many times Anta bumped her. He made sure that he had at least that many love making sessions. On top of this was the babu. The babu had initially used a rubbery substance on his thing and assured her that she wouldn't get pregnant. Yet the rubber fell into disuse as the babu grew intimate and let his guard down. Sibu had a sharp nose (members of Tikna tribe typically had flat noses) which reminded her of the babu's nose.

Biological paternity is a good issue to explore at leisure. The poor have more pressing issues to address: issues of survival. When Sibu was nine, an offer came to buy him off as a domestic help for a good five hundred rupees. That was a time of chaos. Malaria had created havoc and many in the community died of mosquito bites. To make matters worse, both Anta and Saanta were neck deep in debt. This looked like a tempting proposal to both. However Mali would not agree to it. She was especially fond of Sibu. He was a ray of hope in her unremarkable life: a babu born to her. She always believed that this son of hers was destined for greatness. Luckily Anta and Saanta fought over who should get the sale proceed (both claiming to be Sibu's father) and there was a deadlock. Anta sold off one of his other children. Saanta forcibly lay claim over Sibu's younger sister and packed her off to a child trader from Nagpur. He reasoned that she would be happy there getting to work for a rich family, even though he knew very well that Nagpur was a major transit point for female child trafficking.

Sibu faced his first forced displacement when he was twelve. After the establishment of many industries, real estate price in Jeypore and Koraput boomed. Builders made a beeline trying to convert barren and forested land on either side of the highway into gharabari land (private plot). The hamlet in which Sibu grew up was notified as gharabari by the district collectorate without anyone in the village being aware of it.

However, this time around, the resistance was more organised. A militant group, the Maobadi, had spread its tentacles across Western Orissa. From what Sibu had heard, they ran the government in Malkangiri and far south across the Andhra border.

Maobadis were tribals trained in jungle warfare but their leaders were all educated English-speaking outsiders. To spread their movement further, the Maobadis had the territory divided into units and every unit had few of these educated leaders who brought together the youth to agitate on common issues of grievance.

This way the Maobadis – Maoists – spread the germ of revolution. For years now they have been successfully spreading 'class consciousness' among the poor and deprived sections. Their strategy was that of spreading an epidemic. They spread the germ of their ideology in the hearts of the subaltern masses. Their ideologues would come to a village or hamlet, analyse the problems on which collective action was possible, fuel anger among people and make them realise that together they could use violent methods to redress their grievances. Then one day these villagers would come together under the ideologues and attack 'symbols of oppression': government buildings and men in uniform.

There could not be any retaliation as the whole village was involved and a whole village cannot be put behind bars. This way, villagers *learn* to *defy* authority. The ideologues vanish as silently as they had arrived. Police and local administration are left high and dry. The end result was that people get to know – if they unify, they can defy.

Injection, internalisation and acceptance of Maobadi bug completed. Class consciousness created. The village was then marked by a red flag in the Maoist map of India. Once the idea of collective revolt takes root, it persists and grows. As an empowered class with self-consciousness, they shall be potent weapons in the future. The leaders are assured that on the Big Day, the Day of Revolution and Liberation, the village will side with them.

When a builder laid claim over Sibu's hamlet, certain Maoist ideologues from the area got interested. They saw potential in the hamlet. They came and aggressively sold their ideology. The youth got incited. Under the guidance of Maoist leaders, they apprehended the builder's men and roughed them up.

This builder was smart and knew how to handle a Maoist situation. He had good relations with Christian missionaries working in the area. Through them he promised a dispensary and a good education facility to the Dom converts if they agreed to his plan of displacement. The missionaries advocated a relocation looking at the economic benefits. The Doms started taking a pro-displacement stand.

The hamlet got divided on religious lines. Tiknas accused the Doms of treachery. Doms chided Tiknas about their short-sightedness. Someone claimed that Christian gods were civilised and educated; Dharama, the Tikna God, has never gone outside the forests. This infuriated the Tiknas.

A shaman of Tiknas claimed that Dharama had come in her dreams and revealed the truth about Christian gods. All Christians are greedy and evil. The way Christian missionaries bribed Doms to convert, the builder bribes Christian gods. That's why they supported displacement. This infuriated the Doms.

A priest from a nearby church came over and explained that no Dom had ever been converted with enticement. The job of the missionary was only to show the right path. Whether to follow it or not depended entirely upon the individual. He assembled few Tikna youth and explained that Dharama was a false God. If he was a true God, why could he not help his devotees? Why was their condition wretched and deteriorating by the day? If they took the right path, explained the priest, their children would get free education and missionaries would help them get employed. New shawls and dresses would be supplied to them on Christmas Eve every year.

The priest was a convincing speaker and had started to make sense to some Tiknas. But he made the mistake of repeating again and again that Dharama was a false God. A stone propped up from somewhere and hit him in the eye. Following the lead, some conservative elements in the crowd also hurled stones at him. Then the Doms hurled stones at the Tiknas. Then the Tiknas hurled stones at Doms. Kids thought the elders were playing a game of hurling stones and eagerly joined in. Children – both Doms and Tiknas – chased the priest around and hurled stones at him.

The air in their hamlet was charged with communal sentiments. The stone-hurling incident was reported in local papers as a 'riot'. As a result, police patrol increased in the area. This posed a threat to the Maoist ideologues. If one group sided with them, they knew the other would turn informers for the police and report their activities to the authorities. They had to flee in a hurry.

Now that the Maoists had left, it became easy for the builder to play divide and rule. There were a couple of rallies, a few NGO-organised protest marches in front of the district magistrate's office, and minor skirmishes between pro-displacement and resistant groups, but ultimately the hamlet was uprooted. The pro-displacement group got generous rehabilitation packages but the resistant group was left high and dry. Sibu had sided with the resistants. He and his mother had to relocate to a makeshift hamlet nearby. At this place, his mother breathed her last. Mali died of malaria. He was the last of the family by her side at her deathbed. All his siblings had gone; either been sold off or married away, or had resorted to distress migration. Both Anta and Saanta had deserted the family and moved afar in search of work.

After Mali's death, there was no one Sibu had to take care of. There was no reason for him to stay there. Sibu had no idea where to go, what to do. He was not educated, had rarely been out of the hamlet – only to Jeypore town twice to attend seasonal fairs. A friend suggested they board the train and go to the big City. There is a job for everyone in the City and no one is left hungry, his friend had reasoned. Sibu was then only fifteen.

City of Splendour and Subhumans

The City was no kinder to Sibu. He and his companion tried to search for folks from their village or nearby villages, but all in vain. The City was a huge, mobile mass of humans that would remind one of a turbulent sea. There were people from everywhere: Bihar, UP, Jharkhand, Andhra, places which Sibu had never heard of and could never visualise in relation to Koraput. Neither Sibu nor his friend knew any language other than a local dialect of Santhali. Yet they managed to get in touch with an Oriya jobber who got them work at a construction site.

Sibu's compatriot was overwhelmed by the madness of city life and decided to go back.

"Where to?" Sibu asked, to which he had no answer. Yet he was sure he wanted to go back.

"If there is no hope here or there, I better rot there," he said in response to Sibu's persuasion to give the City a chance. He left, leaving Sibu alone with the millions that populate the City.

Sibu was also tempted to leave. He was afraid of being left alone. Yet there were some things about the City – the high rises, the train of vehicles on roads, the enticing women in fashionable attire – that captivated Sibu. The City was a movie running live, and he felt if there was no hope to cling to, this was a better place to rot.

Sibu had managed a place for himself under a flyover. All the others sharing the hole with him were migrants from Bihar. For some time there was peace. With the wages from the construction site, he could manage two square meals. He had made friends with some other workers in the area. He learnt to communicate in Hindi. With his savings he could also arrange a shack and blankets for winter. When the cold became too harsh to bear, he would take a good dose of ganja and that would do the trick.

Few winters passed. During one winter, which turned out to be the coldest in many years, the City was hosting an international meet of industrialists. Policy makers had realised that hosting the event would highlight the City's willingness to facilitate foreign investments. During a survey of the City, the chairman of the organising committee of the international meet saw hovels on pavements, by the roadside, and under flyovers. He was horrified. He was projecting the City as Singapore and this was what the reality of the City was! He soon brought it to the notice of the Mayor.

The Mayor was already frustrated with the migration issue. These migrants were responsible for all the evils the City was suffering from: crime, litter, and eve-teasing. Yet he was always stopped from taking action because of political considerations. This was the right time to act. Since the City's and the country's prestige depended on how grand the City looked in the eyes of multinational companies, this alone was a strong reason to act. He gave a strong directive to the municipal commissioner.

The municipal commissioner, a man of efficiency and diligence, wiped the City clean in just seven days. After seven days he boasted that a tourist visiting the City wound not see anything unpleasant on pavements, roadsides or under bridges and flyovers.

When these tramps were herded away, a few managed to find accommodation in slums. But most of them had to move out to places far from the city centre. Given the high transportation cost, they could not move to and fro between the city centre and the peripheries. So, most lost their jobs.

Unlike other migrants who had compatriots to fall back on, Sibu did not have any kith or kin to help him out during this hour of need. He could not afford to lose his job. So he came back to the city. Twice he tried to set up a shack in dark corners where he thought the municipal and police authorities could not find him and both times he was traced, beaten to pulp, and kicked out.

Sibu had no escape from the wintry nights. The open sky was both home and prison. Sibu took refuge in ganja. The wonder drug worked wonders, but affected his work. Under the influence of marijuana, he lost the strength for the rigours of construction work. Having always believed in the financial principle of hand-to-mouth, soon he fell into an emaciation loop. When even ganja became unaffordable, he became absolutely defenceless against the wrath of winter. To be fair to Sibu, he cannot be entirely blamed for the appalling behaviour he would demonstrate in days to come: a hungry man is a slave of his stomach.

One night, when Sibu was lying by a desolate road in this deplorable condition, a car passing by stopped a few metres away from Sibu and two young men came out of the car. A beautiful young damsel – her fair thighs boasting of the mysteries that lay hidden inside the flashy mini-skirt – also came out of the car. All of them were drunk, but one man was especially so. He could not even stand. He vomited on the roadside while the other man and the beautiful girl lent him their shoulders for support. After that he was deposited in the back seat of the car. He was shouting something in English all the while.

After the car left, a dog came running to check out on the puke. Sibu had been a witness to the scene. He had started dreaming about mating with this young, scantily-dressed woman. In his condition he found great solace in dreams. However, the sudden movement of the dog jolted him out of his reverie and he instinctively shooed the dog away. Then he dragged himself closer and had a look at the puke. He could see undigested pieces of cottage cheese and chicken in the vomit. The man had evidently had too much food with his drinks, and had not chewed the food properly, Sibu observed. He looked left and right, and to his back. There was no one, none but the stray dog greedily eyeing the vomit. Sibu cautiously went for a piece of chicken. It tasted good. He tried to remember when he had eaten chicken the last time.

There was obviously an abhorring smell to the puke, but after a while Sibu got used to it. He devoured the chicken and cheese pieces and still his craving was not satisfied. He went down on his knees and started eating the liquid concoction while the stray enviously looked on. Who knows when the next feast would be – and whether there would be another in this lifetime.

The feast was opulent and Sibu also got a feel of the foreign liquor that was in the puke. That night, under the dark sky and yellow glow of street lamps, Sibu wondered why man did not eat vomit.

Sibu was reminded of his childhood, and how his mother used to reprimand him when he picked any food from the ground. As far as his memory went, he always went out into the forests to defecate. In his hamlet he and his friends would go into the woods together early in the morning, defecate there and then would go to a nearby pond to bathe and clean. But his kid brother used to defecate in the veranda itself (before he became of age to go into the woods). He fondly remembered how his kid brother would defecate, then stick a finger into his light yellow potty and put some into his mouth. Then someone would notice and yell for their mother, who would come and force the potty out from his mouth and wash him.

Sibu's thoughts drifted to his mother, his siblings and the hamlet. How safe he was in his mother's care, in spite of the vagaries of destiny they had to endure! He longed for those innocent days. How did he land up in this state? A tear rolled down his eye as he dreamt of his mother affectionately applying oil to his hair. It was another lifetime. Now his hair was dry, dirty, and rough.

Sleep seldom comes to an empty stomach. That day sleep did not come to Sibu till early in the morning in spite of the fulsome dinner. And before his eyes closed he had concluded that if a stray dog could live a life of style under the naked sky and without a job, so could he! It is the acculturation of human behaviour that forbids a man from living like a dog. It was his mother who forbade him from eating puke. But had she herself ever tasted puke? Sibu slept an enlightened slumber, having discovered out a secret art of living.

In the following days Sibu faced another hurdle in his quest for food: puke, it seems, was not readily available. So he diversified into leftovers. He had managed to find a big hotel where lots of young people came and stayed till late in the night. Unlike most hotels, the staff of this hotel directly threw out the leftovers in gutters. Sibu kept rummaging in the gutters and the garbage dumps outside the hotel and usually managed to get some food. Hotel security was lax and security personnel were oblivious to Sibu's trespassing. Weekends offered bonanza leftovers, for many young men and women would come and party all night in the hotel's discotheque.

Sibu had always been fascinated by the girls who visited the hotel at night. They were beautiful and came in all sorts of funny clothes. Sibu did not complain as long as they revealed their slender legs and luscious cleavages. The discotheque generally closed at three past midnight and many of these young women would come out in a drunken state. Some would be dancing wildly just outside the exit gate; yet others would openly fondle their male partners. Sibu often lingered about the hotel late on weekends and ogled at the girls from behind a garbage bin.

One unfortunate night Sibu was caught ogling at a voluptuous girl by her male partners. She seemed to have come with three male friends and they were having a hard time controlling her. With a cigarette in one hand and a can of beer in the other, she danced wildly as her male friends dragged her to a cab. At this point one of them saw Sibu staring at her. Drunk that he was, he grew aggressive and pulled Sibu from behind the garbage bin. Then the three of them started beating him. Soon after, a few other boys joined them. A bony girl in a red skirt also came by and cheered the boys working their feet on Sibu. After they roughed him up, hotel security grabbed Sibu, slapped him hard and warned him not to come anywhere near the hotel again.

The bodily pain was unbearable. One of the boys was wearing hard army shoes and he kept kicking on Sibu's chest. His half-torn sweater was now torn into shreds. Worse, he had lost access to a source of nutritious leftovers. The achievement of having managed to peek into the bony girl's skirt while he was being roughed up was not much of a consolation.

Yuckman Begins

The biographer wonders: is the reader disgusted enough? Is the reader exclaiming "yuck!"? Is the reader impulsively considering throwing this biography into a dustbin? The story of Sibu may not have the luxury of space in most bookshelves. It is a distasteful narrative, nevertheless, it is a powerful one and deserves narration. His world was an eco-system of abject misery and inhuman conditions, justice to which a chronicler cannot do without taking recourse to explicit, vivid description. Howsoever gross.

And if not yet sufficiently grossed over by the chronicle of Yuckman, one must brace herself or himself for the shit that is to come. Real shit. Pure shit. Deep shit. Literally.

Since the day Sibu first ate puke, the idea of tasting shit had taken root in his mind. Shit was like an enigma to him... *there is shit all around*. Everyone shits. Infants starts shitting the moment they come into the world. An octogenarian with one foot already in the realm of spirits squats during a daily session of shitting. Man shits. Dog shits. Bovines shit. All the great leaders shit. The flawless divas of the City also shit. The great God Dharama, the almighty, also shits.

In the story of Dharama and Andharia, Andharia lived in the early days when there was no night and Sun's rays blessed Earth perpetually. Andharia was once collecting firewood in the forest. Suddenly he came face to face with Dharama, who was defecating deep in the jungle assured that no one would come by. He found it humiliating that a mortal caught Him in such a position. He cursed mankind with darkness (*andharia* is the Tikna word for darkness, after Andharia). He ordained that day would be followed by night when man would rest and not disturb the Gods and spirits of forefathers – vagrants of the woods – who come out in the night.

Faeces is waste of the food that body has rejected. It is after all food and can fill an empty stomach. The words by which faeces was described sounded negative to Sibu. So he gave a new name to faeces: "amrit". Amrit is nectar. In the coming days Sibu often wondered how it would be if amrit was collected, spiced up with flavours and aroma, and recycled as biscuits. Or cakes. Amrit of a diarrhoeic nature could be recycled as a drink. How easily could that eradicate the problem of starvation!

Having made up his mind, early one morning Sibu went towards the railway siding running behind a small slum. People of the slum lightened themselves up by the railway siding every morning. This morning Sibu rummaged through the faeces. The amrit he would taste had to be fresh; stale amrit contained insects. Soon he came upon a dark yellowish mass of amrit. After making sure that no one was looking, he took little bit in his finger and tasted it. He felt like vomiting and made up his mind not to voyage further into this experiment. Fickle that he was, after a moment he came back to the amrit mass, took the mass in his hands, formed a laddu out of it, and gulped it. This time there was no nausea.

In the days that followed, Sibu took his experiment to a new level. On pre-determined days he would take amrit and only amrit. He found that eating amrit satiated hunger immediately, but then after an hour, he'd again feel hungry. While hunting for fresh amrit, he also got a revelation that amrit told a lot about the defecator's food habits. If the food was not uniformly digested, it showed in the amrit. Amrit showed how disciplined a man was in his eating habits and eating times. If someone ate a lot of junk, his amrit had a strong foul smell. Overeating and swallowing reflected in undigested food pieces in amrit.

Amrit also stated a lot about the defecator's personality. If the amrit was uniformly spread over the ground it shows stability and confidence of the man squatting. On the other hand, if someone shat in fits and bounds, thus creating cascades of amrit rolls on the ground, it indicated fickle-mindedness.

Having succeeded in conquering the needs of his stomach, Sibu now started experimenting with new food stuff. This, I believe, was an error and probably what Sibu did next led to the unfortunate circumstances that followed.

Few sponge iron plants in the outskirts of the city discharged industrial wastes into a fresh water lake. By the norms of the pollution control board, these wastes had to be adequately treated and disposed off. That being the costlier option, these sponge iron plants usually discharged the wastes into the lake. Over time, the water in the lake had turned black. Marine life had vanished long ago. Migratory birds also skipped the lake during their yearly tour. Dark masses of foul smelling wastes had accumulated in various corners. Toxicity had increased to such a level that even mangrove trees could not survive.

Many slums were located across the perimeter of the lake. Slums meant a lot of shitting in the open and shitting meant a lot of food for Sibu. Sibu had come here for shit, but something drew him towards the lake. After a gratifying lunch of shit, he stripped himself and took a plunge in the dark depths. He tasted the water and tried to comprehend its taste. It tasted salty, but not bad.

After Sibu came out of the lake, he had a severe headache. Putting on his bare clothing, he lay down by the lake under the winter sun. After sometime he felt a strange stimulation – a feeling of exhilaration much different from the high he had experienced from ganja or local liquor. His body was paralysed and he lay there for hours thinking, dreaming, and laughing.

Few hours later when the effect of lake water had subsided, he got up and drank some more water. Then he sat under a tree and went into a deep slumber.

Sibu seldom moved out of the lake area. He would bathe in the lake, eat as and when he pleased, and dream of the inebriating lake water.

At the onset of summer, Sibu was afflicted by a strange skin disease. Pores started appearing on his skin. His skin itched a lot and was turning abnormally hard. These pores spread all over his body and face. Sibu was clueless about what he could do or whom he could approach for help. He also developed a craving for the lake's toxicity. Notwithstanding the pain the skin disease gave him, a good bath in the lake and a hearty supper of shit made the discomfort go.

Curious things were happening to Sibu's body. While Sibu did realise this, he could not comprehend what to do about it. Within a month of pores developing on his skin, he realised that he was having some stomach issues. His insides were burning; it was as if an oven had been incinerated inside his stomach. With every breath, he suffered an irritation in his nasal cavity.

He moved away from the slum area to a part of the lake perimeter vegetated by mangroves. Here he found respite from the summer heat; yet he had no clue as to how to deal with the heat within. He also realised that he was feeling light – literally. There seemed to be not only an oven but also a huge hot air balloon in his stomach, which pushed him up.

At first Sibu doubted that one of the forest gods had possessed him. When the pores first appeared, he thought Sitala, the chicken pox goddess had possessed him. Then when his stomach started burning he was convinced that no power less wicked than Goddess Chandi could have possessed him. He understood that such illness could not be fathomed by any doctor. He needed the help of a shaman. But where would he find a shaman in the City?

All Sibu did was lie down and pray. Sibu did not know any chants, but he remembered a prayer to the Lord Dharama that his mother had taught him. His condition worsened; Sibu realised that he had become paralysed in a few days' time. He could not move any part of his body, nor could he drag himself towards some shit. Inside the mangrove territory and with a dry tongue, Sibu could not even give a distress call to slum dwellers.

Sibu lay paralysed for more than a month, without food or liquid. In this period, all he did was pray to the benevolent Lord Dharama and beg for reprieve from the Goddess Chandi.

He could also feel the mischief that Goddess Chandi was doing with his body. He could feel his blood drying out. His heart beat faster, much faster than usual. His nose was also playing tricks with him. It had grown into a funnel and emitted a strange gas in short gusts. One day when a dog was sniffing at his body, his nose emitted the gas and the dog died instantly. As for breathing, he had stopped using his nasal zone for breathing long back. The soreness that came with every breath had become intolerable. He discovered that the pores on his skin did effective breathing, sparing him the suffering. Once in four to five hours, black acidic liquid would come out of these pores and flow down. Such was the toxicity of this liquid that when it flowed onto a bush, the bush desiccated in hours.

After almost a month in this state, Sibu woke up one evening to find that he could move. In fact, he felt strong and energetic. The strange fever that had attacked him in fits subsided all of a sudden. This was nothing but the deeds of Dharama. When Goddess Chandi attacks you, She is slow and steady in inflicting pain. It also takes a lot of power to make Her leave you. If She leaves so suddenly, it can be only when Lord Dharama expresses His displeasure. Dharama, the Just and Kind, had listened to his prayers.

Sibu's felicity was but short-lived. When he peeped into the lake, he was shocked to see a monster – the ugliest being he had ever seen. The very sight of the monster frightened him. It was only when his fright showed on the face of the lake monster that he realised he was looking at his own reflection.

Muck and Mayhem

Five months have passed since the first reported sighting of the monster they now call 'Yuckman'. There has been no marked progress in the investigations on this modern day monster. Opinions are divided on his existence, his persistence and motives. Five public sightings of Yuckman have been reported, three of these at shopping malls. All the malls in the City have now closed shop, apprehending another attack on malls. The first major attack of Yuckman was on a discotheque. Subsequently most hotels in the City have stopped entertaining late night parties.

The main problem our law enforcement agencies face is that there is no precedence of a creature remotely resembling this monster in recorded history. He is fast and fatal. He wreaks havoc and leaves the spot before the police can arrive. Even if field formations could corner him in future, they are worried that they do not know his powers in entirety. How are they going to trap him? How will they contain him?

More importantly, *what* is this being? *Where* does it come from? *Where* does it vanish? These are questions that remain unanswered even after five attacks (every single eye witness has been interviewed at great length).

The Mayor comes panicking, requesting me to help in the investigations. I hear he has been requesting many other experts to find answers. The man has been taking a lot of heat lately. Business houses have incurred huge losses because of the Yuckman panic. The consumer class has demonstrated the most erratic behaviour since the toxic creature's surge. Tourism has thinned. Business houses have offered to help financially, as long as a quick solution is reached at.

I am a retired researcher. I was one of the first researchers in the country in the field of biochemistry. When research in genetic engineering picked up, I was again one of the first few researchers. Yet, these specialised fields of study have fast advanced since my retirement. I am not in touch with current research and latest trends.

I express my shortcomings to the Mayor, but he is adamant. He wants everyone, who may be of any help, to work on Yuckman. I am enrolled in a committee of experts headed by Dr A.K. Sinha, a senior professor of IIT Kharagpur. The committee meets every Monday and Friday in the conference room of a posh hotel (which anyways stays unoccupied because of the Yuckman scare).

The committee's agenda in the first meeting is to give the creature a name. After much deliberation the committee short-lists four names: The Dirty Devil, The Shit Monger, The Filthy Fiend, and The Toxic Troll. The issue is deliberated upon in the second meeting, but the committee cannot make any headway.

The police commissioner, who happens to be the ex-officio secretary of the committee, proposes a new name his son had suggested to him: Shit-Man. The chairman, Sinha, and police commissioner have a difference of opinion over giving such a simplistic name to the creature. They have a heated argument over the issue. Some members speculate a power tussle between the chairman and secretary over who controls the high profile committee.

I see myself as the most inactive member of the committee. When proposals were called for to name the monster, I could not contribute a single name. But I don't complain. I have been provided with a chauffeur-driven vehicle, certain funds for my investigations (which will not be audited), and two clerks for secretarial support.

I feel guilty about my lack of involvement. After one of the committee's post-meeting lunches, I pick up a preliminary report on The Filthy Fiend (this has finally been accepted as official name of the monster) and read it through.

There have been five public sightings of Yuckman, all in different areas of the City. The first sighting was in an industrial area. Yuckman was found wandering around a lake. None of the persons who vow that they have seen him can accurately describe him. They just say that he looked ugly, real ugly. They in fact called him a demon and threw stones at him. One onlooker said that Yuckman wanted to talk to them. When he was shooed away, he rose (high) in the air and landed on the roof of a shack. Then he jumped around the slum settlement (he could easily jump fifteen feet above ground level) and spat faeces from his mouth. Then he jumped into the lake and disappeared.

The second sighting was in a night club in one of the reputed hotels of the City. Yuckman attacked at around one in the night. CCTV cameras installed in the hotel lobby caught the first sight of Yuckman as he entered the building and killed a few security personnel with gas ejections. He went in and got hold of young women dancing on the dance floor. His attack was so sudden that everyone was taken by surprise. He did not seem to have any specific target or purpose. He arbitrarily got hold of people and killed them. Eyewitnesses say he emitted poisonous gases which instantly killed many people.

It seems he had cornered few young women dancing in the club. It was pretty dark inside the club hence none of the eye witnesses could give a clear picture of what he was doing. The women were petrified and huddled together in a corner. He danced around them in a mad frenzy and sprinkled shit-water on them. Many women reported molestation bids made by Yuckman. He managed to strip a few of the women.

One woman tried to run away, unable to bear the smell, and the disgusting apparition in front of her. Yuckman took two jumps and positioned himself at the pub's exit. He stopped the woman and shouted at her in a tongue no one could understand. His voice was rough and patchy. Further, he had a strange accent and no one was sure what language he spoke. He moved towards the woman chiding her, his yellow eyes protruding out and his yellow teeth smelling severely. The woman tried to run away from him. He grabbed her by her arms, put one hand inside her blouse, and licked her cheek. Her fair face was painted yellow by his shit saliva (this part is vividly mentioned in the report). He then forced his tongue into her mouth. Small streams of shit saliva leaked down the woman's throat while Yuckman's tongue penetrated deep into her cavity.

The woman excreted in fright. Yuckman smelled excreta. She was wearing a skirt which did not impede Yuckman's way. Spreading her legs apart, Yuckman tore off her underwear and devoured her excreta. He licked her bottom and then sucked into her arse hole to ensure that he had not missed even a bit of her excreta. Then he stood up and catching the woman by her neck, brought her face close to his and mumbled something. One of the witnesses stated to the police that he was complementing her on the taste of her excreta while all other witnesses vouched that they could not make sense of his voice.

He then lifted the woman, placed her on his shoulder and walked out of the hotel. Anyone who tried to stop him was put to death with gas emissions from his body parts.

The police arrived after Yuckman had left. There was a repulsive stench of rotten eggs coming out of the gutters which drained the police sick. A day later, after the gutters were cleaned, dead bodies of the missing security guards were found.

Fourteen men and three women had died in the carnage. A few victims' faces had been permanently damaged by Yuckman's acid attacks.

Given the extent of the damage caused by that event, law enforcement agencies were under immense pressure to bring the culprit to book. The police department, as it appears from the detailed report, remained clueless as to the identity of this mysterious individual with supernatural powers (he was still not christened as Yuckman). This time informers also could not help. Their best bet was that this was a person with pathological traits. He had attacked the disco masquerading in a frightening costume in the middle of the night to spread panic.

Police investigation always circles around a motive. When they cannot find any, they usually brand the perpetrator a psychopath, so said a columnist in *City Post*. The *Post* had its own version of the massacre. It contended that DRDO, the research arm of defence ministry, has been working on a secret project to develop lethal soldiers with superpowers. Towards this end they recruit men from the army and test various drugs on them. This activity is carried out clandestinely in a secret facility just outside city limits. Our competent scientists did manage to develop super-soldiers but could not control them. One of the side effects of ability-enhancing drugs is that many test subjects lose their mind. One of these super-soldiers managed to escape from the DRDO facility and made his way into the disco. Later the DRDO personnel managed to apprehend him and take him back to the facility. The police could not make any headway into the matter because of defence ministry's pressure tactics.

The right wing paper *The Daily Satsang*, run by the City Sunwarsevak Sangh (CSS) decreed that the perpetrator was the avatar of Lord Krishna. In this age of Kali, when people have forgotten all propriety and women all shame, Kalki – the avatar of Krishna – had come to remind people of Indian culture. He would clean this world of all the degenerative elements that have corrupted the morals of the society. One opinion in the newspaper was that these women who hang around in discos at midnight, drink and smoke, deserved the punishment meted out to them. Another columnist stated that Lord Krishna – symbol of purity – had embraced human shit and other polluting material for only by embracing muck can he fight the muck of this age. This attack on the disco demonstrated that unruly, uncultured, characterless, shameless, loose women would be punished for their unruly, uncultured, characterless, shameless, loose behaviour.

Opinions aired in *The Daily Satsang* were met with angry reactions. Feminists went on to denounce its views as chauvinist and orthodox. The *City Girls' Bing*, a weekly tabloid, launched the *Bra utaro campaign* to assert women's independence and self-determination to the bigots. One fine Sunday, participants of this campaign met and marched to the offices of *The Daily Satsang* and CSS, flipped open their brassieres and flung them at CSS sevaks. In protests outside the residence of the CSS Sarsanghchalak (head of the organisation), he was dared to call his Kalki to prevent women from undressing in public. The octogenarian came out to pacify the women. When the ladies participating in the protest threw the brassieres at him, he got captivated by the sight of their beautiful bosoms and stared at the women lasciviously. This further infuriated the protesters who then roughed him up, unclothed him, and dressed him in a pink panty and bra.

The City Express, known for its long history of investigative journalism, came up with the revelation that the disco was owned in proxy by a notorious underworld don who was now basking in the sun on the shores of Thailand. He had been involved in a bloody gang war with a rival gang for months now. *The City Express* opined that the rival gang had hired a butcher to attack this felon's business premises.

The term 'Yuckman' was first used in an Amul butter advertisement. In this advertisement the Amul girl, a man with shit coming out of his mouth, and a few kids hungrily eye a pack of Amul butter. The subtext read:

No one can resist
Be he malicious or religious
Not even Yuckman, nor any scatologist

Utterly, butterly, delicious
AMUL : The Taste of India

After the night club incident, Yuckman was spotted thrice – at regular intervals – in shopping malls. Since malls were well-lit buildings, soon a clearer picture of Yuckman could be arrived at. CCTV recordings from these malls were brought into the police headquarters and analysed in detail. It was seen from the recordings that Yuckman was tall and dark. Nay, black. Jet black in colour, to be specific. He had pachydermatous skin, unlike any other human, and there were pores all over his body. The pores emitted acids and it appeared the creature had control over the acidic emissions from his skin. His nose was not a nose but an anterior elongation of his face, more like a pig's snout. His fingernails and eye balls were yellow in colour (the same shade human faeces usually have) and shit saliva flowed off his mouth. In his mall attacks he was wearing a white linen sheet wrapped over his upper body unlike in the first appearance in which he was naked except for a loin cloth. One end of the linen was tucked into his brown coloured three-quarters, while the other end was draped over his right shoulder like the loose end of a sari. Few witnesses claimed that he was bald below the hood, although CCTV footages clearly show stray hair filaments on his otherwise bald head. Though he had a slim frame, his torso was unusually swollen and looked like a huge cylinder.

Post-mortem reports of his victims indicated that the pores on his body emitted a gas that had traces of Phosgene, Chlorine, Chloromethyl Chloroformate, and Chloropicrin, which are toxic. His pig nose ejected methane and propane gases which are highly inflammable.

On closer study I find that there is a pattern to his madness. He usually attacks crowded places and kills people at whim: by emitting poisonous gases from his skin-pores and nose. His wrists and ankles are unusually swollen. They are capable of ejecting jets of acidic liquid, (the nature of which is not clear from reports) which he revels in throwing at young women's faces. He seizes money from shop counters, but that is not his primary purpose. He creates mayhem with a missionary zeal. It appears he takes some kind of sadistic pleasure by killing young men and disfiguring young women. The worst victims of his attacks are security guards who face sorry deaths.

Yuckman is quick. He enters, damages, and flees in a blitzkrieg operation. Every time he attacks, he abducts a woman. Not one of the four women he has abducted till date has been found. Why does he abduct these women? I look at their photos and see that they are beautiful women in their late teens. Does he abduct them to satisfy his carnal desires?

After finishing the report, my ratiocination drive me to some conclusions about Yuckman. He is not a beast. Beasts do not loot cash counters. Only humans with a history of social life understand the value of money. It is also interesting to note that he prefers looting shopping malls over banks or jewellery stores.

Secondly, he is driven by hedonistic impulses. The report has stressed that Yuckman attacks without any rational motive. This is because the report has been prepared by the police and it is difficult for the policemen to comprehend Yuckman as a man. They have started with the basic assumption that this is a monstrous beast.

A worrying trend can be seen from the three mall attacks: Yuckman has been improvising. His abilities to focus his liquid and gaseous emissions on his victims had improved. His agility has improved over time. Yuckman could easily scale a height of twenty-five to thirty feet when he jumped now, while he hadn't looked sure of himself in his initial attacks. Now he manoeuvred freely, making good use of his nimble competences.

The Filthy Fiend

Sibu sized himself up in a mirror and chuckled at his ugliness. A beautiful, fair, voluptuous young woman with long jet black hair was lying in the adjacent room. Much as she despised Sibu and had feigned fright and disgust, she could not hide the satisfaction Sibu gave her.

Sibu had picked her up at a shopping mall. It had been Sibu's fourth raid, and the third on a mall. Sibu had picked a woman in each of his earlier raids. He would find a new place to confine each one. Sibu would keep the woman for a couple of weeks and mate with her. He would then dump the girl.

His intention was never to pet a woman. He knew the vagaries of maintaining a pet... she has to be taken care of; she would need a home; and invariably women were disgusted with him. Sibu found it convenient to find a new woman and a new nest, copulate with her and then let her go. Off she'd go and Sibu would get time out for his vagrant grazing around sewers, garbage, and waste dump yards (ever since his transformation, his appetite had increased many folds).

Sibu was, however, not insensitive. In his previous kidnaps, he had realised that the woman picked got frightened and disgusted not only by his looks, but also by the places he established his nest in. To stay safely away from human population, he would find a place deep inside an abandoned mine pit or a barren plot surrounded by garbage dumps and place his prize woman there. One of the women had complained that there was no AC. Another had cribbed that the nest did not have a good 'ambience'. Sibu believed that giving his captives the comfort of a house would dilute their frigidity towards him.

This time Sibu established his nest in a middle class residential area. He had sneaked in and blown out lethal gas from his snout on the lone old couple staying there. He installed his new girl in the bedroom and fucked her day in and day out. Initially she was frigid. She would frown at him and cry like a baby. In a few days she got accustomed to the shit and other smelly fluids that drivelled from Sibu's body. Then she had in fact become responsive to Sibu. Sibu drilled into her with such passionate force and consistency that she could not, at times, hide her orgasmic joy.

And now the beautiful woman was sleeping in the adjacent room, rejuvenating herself for his next fuck. A grin appeared on Sibu's reflection in the mirror, which he thought made him look more eerie. He was reminded of the first time he had seen his ugliness in a lake's reflection. That time he had been frightened. He had wondered what sin could he have committed to incite Goddess Chandi to curse him with this deformity. He was deformed beyond identity.

Ashamed of his condition, he had initially cohered to his lake habitat. In a few days he realised that when Goddess Chandi had left his body, she had left behind a powerful demon inside him. Some of the demon's powers he was still discovering. Just a fortnight back he had realised that the gas coming out of his nose was inflammable. It caught fire. He had then conducted an experiment inside a huge garbage tank. He blew out from his nose with all the force he could muster and then lit the propulsion with a matchstick. It had turned into a huge jet of fire.

Looking at himself in the mirror, Sibu was reminded of the tale of Dharama and Sitala, the chicken pox goddess. Sitala was the great god Dharama's favourite mistress. He was fonder of her than even his wife Durugi. Sitala was beautiful and tender. She was younger than any of Dharama's mistresses. Dharama would spend time with her for days together, till his phallus turned sour. Other mistresses were ignored. They grew jealous of Sitala so they hatched a conspiracy. When Durugi had gone to visit her parents' village, they spread a rumour that Dharama planned to marry Sitala and turn Durugi into a mere mistress.

When the rumour fell on Durugi's ears, she rejected it as a mere rumour. Durugi knew that Dharama and Durugi were dual manifestations of a single divine origin. They had separate existence, yet were inseparable. Dharama, the Lord of Justice, walked the woods to ascertain equity and balance. He meted justice to everyone: man, beast, flora, and the mountains. Durugi was the goddess of harmony. She bestowed spirits with peace and satiation. She synthesised all life forces into the complex juxtapose that our nature is. It was by the continued intercourse of Dharama and Durugi that stability came to this world.

Three lies make a truth. When the rumour spread in Durugi's natal village, she lost face. She started believing that Dharama indeed harboured intentions of leaving her and marrying Sitala. Though a goddess, she was after all a woman and it is in the nature of women to question the intentions of husbands. She sent a messenger to ask Dharama to visit her at her mother's house. Dharama did not respond. That infuriated her further.

Summoning the most powerful of spirits into her, she turned into the dreaded Chandi form. After becoming Chandi, she danced in hysteria for three days and three nights. In these three days, many villages were destroyed by Chandi's fury. Dense forests were grounded. Each thump of her feet was followed by an earthquake in a distant village.

When Chandi had started her phrenetic dance ritual, many gods and goddesses had approached Dharama and requested him to appease her. But Dharama had roared that he did not care for a woman who did not trust him. His male ego prevented him from going to her. After three days of mayhem, he finally agreed to appease her.

Dharama managed to stop Chandi's dance ritual. Dharama then took Chandi into a hut and overcame her. Chandi was a violent lover but lost much of her strength during coitus. Dharama had expected that after making love Chandi would regress to Durugi. But that was not to happen. Chandi was now relaxed, but did not forget her purpose. She dragged Dharama out of the hut and addressing her natal village and the revered Mother Tree as witness said that Sitala has to be punished for trying to disturb the Dharama-Durugi unity. Chandi cursed: May Sitala be deformed beyond recognition, may her beauty become a myth and her famed delicacy a matter of jape. Only then will I regress.

It pained Dharama that Sitala was cursed for no apparent fault of hers. He could have saved Sitala from the curse, but then Chandi would destroy the balance of nature. Chandi had already caused severe damage and he could not afford to take the risk. So he let Sitala turn ugly and deformed.

However, after Chandi had regressed to Durugi and Durugi had forgiven him, Dharama blessed Sitala with powers of a goddess spirit. From that day on, Sitala roamed the habitats of those who sinned and possessed the sinners. Health workers said the patient had been afflicted by chicken pox, but it was actually Goddess Sitala who possessed the patient. She punishes those who have erred; yet benevolent that she is, she leaves the person in a few weeks with not more than a few marks. If the man has committed grave crimes, her marks remain on him for the rest of his life and remind him of those crimes.

Sitala lost her famed beauty, even her identity as a human when Chandi cursed her. Dharama, who was so fond of her, did not give her a single glance after she became deformed. Yet this unfortunate turn of events made her strong and immortal.

Sibu wondered if Dharama had similar designs for him. Months back, he was weak and pitiful. He was a victim of destiny. His purpose in life was to survive; and what for to survive? Such questions of philosophy did not occur to him when in a state of hunger. He was a helpless spectator to the course of his life. He was but a speck of dust that travelled wherever the breeze took him. He coursed with the flux of destiny, floating across the huge expanse of time without any say of his own.

But not anymore.

Has my streak of bad luck ended? Sibu wondered. Sibu's mother Mali had lost faith in Dharama, the Just One, during her last days. She had wondered why Dharama had been so cruel to her people. She would even curse Dharama, saying that he had become greedy. The company people, builders and traders were rich. Perhaps he was softened by their indulgences and offerings and had turned against his poor devotees.

Dharama doles justice in mysterious ways, which humans are not privy to. Sibu was convinced that he had been redeemed. Dharama had given him extraordinary powers in return for a lifelong journey of pain and suffering. He was no longer an object of pity or decry; no longer a *victim* of circumstances. He was now an active agent in his life.

Sibu reared out of his reverie on hearing the sound of glass breaking. He peeped into the bedroom to find his mistress flustered. A vase had crashed on the floor by the bed. On seeing him she expressed an unusually kind smile. She spread out her legs and invited him in with a seductive smile.

When Sibu had bumped her for the first time, she had a shaved pubis. Now she had turned bushy, and the bush between the spread legs further aroused Sibu. He was about to dash into her when he suddenly wondered why she had suddenly become so coy with him. He wondered why she would entice him to fuck her. Had she got a kick for his fucks? Had he really found a girl who, although it sounded kinky even to him, liked him? Had he found his better half? He has been experiencing too much lately to dismiss the idea, however improbable. Maybe!

Or maybe not! He smelt something fishy. He pulled his mistress out of bed and frisked her. Then he checked the bed sheet and pillow. He found a mobile phone inside the pillow cover.

"I found it in the drawer. I just tried to call my mother," the girl explained.

"And did you call the police?" Sibu asked in a hoarse tone and grabbed her neck.

About ten minutes later, policemen broke open the front door and barged in. Each cop had a gun in one hand and a handkerchief pressed to their nose in another. Most of them frowned, evidently finding it hard to bear the smell.

They heard cries for help from the bedroom. A team swiftly moved into the room while others worked on securing the perimeter. In the bedroom, they found a half-naked girl wriggling in pain. Acid had been thrown on her face. Two dead bodies – an old couple – were found in the basement. No one else was found, though the whole house reeked of Yuckman.

Homo Shitens

It is quite easy to decipher Yuckman 'once facts', as available, are separated from fiction (which has been growing by the day, thanks to (a) an active but confused media, (b) scared and speculative citizens, and (c) a police commissioner with a big mouth) and analysed.

Yuckman is a living creature. He has motives. He is hedonistic – his focus is only on women and money. The mayhem he causes every time he strikes is perhaps his exhibition of powers or his ruthless vengeance on civilized society (for whatever reasons) or both.

Yuckman is interested in human females. His cognitive skills are as developed as any other human. Hence logic impels us to come to the conclusion that Yuckman is a human male. A man.

He has superhuman powers. How could he get such powers? He is a **mutant**.

Yuckman is a *living* biogas plant. He consumes organic wastes and processes them to produce Carbon Monoxide (CO) and Methane (CH_4) gases. The gas content in his body reduces his absolute weight. Light gases inside his body make it easier for him to jump over large heights. Biogas reduction process demands huge volumes of biomass (waste). Yuckman must be a voracious eater. Huge volumes of byproduct have to be excreted out on regular intervals. Yuckman's veins has mutated into narrow pipes for excretion. These pipes end up in pores formed on Yuckman's skin. Acidic liquids are excreted from these pores. Excretion also takes place from the mouth, as seen by eyewitnesses at the discotheque raid. Some veins ending up in the skin pores function as gas outlets.

Now the question is: what kind of mutant is he? Was he born like that or *mutated* later in life, owing to extraneous factors? Mutation by birth happens if a genetic mutation happens in the embryo itself. Basically a sperm penetrates an egg to give rise to the embryo. The egg contains one set of twenty-three chromosome strands of the mother. The sperm contains one set of twenty-three chromosome strands of the father. When the sperm fertilizes the egg, the DNA of the father chromosomes physically align with DNA of the mother chromosomes to produce twenty-three pairs of chromosomes that the embryo inherits. After nine months, a child is born containing these twenty-three pairs. Mutations at birth happen when this complicated process goes wrong. There are many medical cases demonstrating errors in the fertilisation process. However, most cases reflect maladaptive mutations, i.e. the mutation leads to physical and cognitive damage in the child. For example, Down's Syndrome, which happens due to errors in this procedure, leads to severe cognitive impairment. Mutation in Yuckman seems to be adaptive, i.e. the mutation in him has enhanced his human skills. Further, the mutation in Yuckman is extreme. It appears that the very genetic codes in his chromosomes have changed drastically.

I believe that Yuckman is not a mutant by birth. If he were, it would have been difficult for his caretakers to keep him hidden from society for so long. Any hospital, in which such a weird child is born, would naturally report it to the health department or the media. There has been no such reporting. Even if we make the assumption that he was a monster child and was kept hidden by his guardians till now, his behaviour does not add up. He is definitely hedonistic, given his lust for women and an eye on rupee notes. Anyone brought up in seclusion would not have had the socialisation that is needed for the lust, or the greed to rise in the first place. If he were born as a monster child, I doubt if he would have identified human females as females of his species.

So Yuckman is definitely a mutant by exposure. I find the most conclusive evidence of his being a mutant from medical reports on Yuckman. The police had collected samples of his hair and salivary remains after his attack on a mall. These were taken to a lab and studied. The genetic structure in his hair cells was found to be different from that in his saliva. The chromosomes in his hair cells are that of a human; doctors could not decipher the genes in his salivary cells, but they are definitely non-human.

Hair cells are dead cells. The genetic codes in his hair represent that of the man before his mutation into Yuckman. Genetic codes in the saliva are that of post-mutation Yuckman. Surprisingly, neither the doctors have stressed on such obvious results, nor has anyone pointed it out. No further analysis of genetic codes has been made.

I also acknowledge how problematic it is to explain transformation of a man into Yuckman. There are known cases of humans mutating on exposure to nuclear and chemical toxins. Victims of the Hiroshima-Nagasaki nuclear bomb blasts and the Bhopal gas tragedy are famous instances (children of such victims have been born with genetic abnormalities). In these cases, only the tissues which were exposed to toxins got mutated. Also the mutation did not follow any functional pattern; they were random. Genetic codes of different tissues of the same victim were affected differently. That's why the changes are usually referred to as 'genetic defects'.

The case of Yuckman is different. Basically different tissues of the human body are specialised in carrying out specialised functions. For example, heart tissues are specialised in pumping blood in and out. Kidney tissues are specialised in cleaning and removal of wastes. The cells in all these tissues contain the same genes (the human individual's genes), but are specialised and hence the genetic codes vary from tissue to tissue. Kidney cells, for example, cannot convert into heart cells. The only cells which can be used to produce any specialised cell are stem cells. In the case of Yuckman, his entire body seems to have been mutated. All specialised tissue cells have been mutated and in their own way. His skin tissues have mutated into an excretory organ and the sweat-pores on his skin function to excrete excessive gases and acids produced by his body. His nose has developed into a pig nose; it is known to pass off another kind of gas. His torso is abnormally large and cylindrical – my guess is that his digestive system has mutated into the organ in which the fermentation of biodegradable matter takes place. Hence mutation in Yuckman is not singular, but multiple. All individual mutations have come together to produce a biogas-plant-mutant. None of the mutations have been maladaptive;

all are adaptive mutations. It is as if a software engineer has written genetic codes in a computer – different codes for different tissue cells – and thus designed a functional human biogas machine; then hardware was brought in the form of a human being and codes were imprinted into the body. If this were to happen by the process of evolution, it would take a couple of thousand years (at the least). How did this evolutionary leap take place? Trying to find an explanation to this in toxins is perplexing.

After rummaging through research literature, I have come across a factor that quite explains the mutation satisfactorily. The causality lies not in toxins but viruses. Viruses are basically infectious agents made up of only genetic material: DNA or RNA. Computer viruses have also been termed so because these are 'cheat codes' that stealthily enter the computer and change its system configuration. Viruses themselves undergo genetic changes quite frequently. Being codes of DNA and RNA, many viruses have the ability to 'overwrite' genetic codes of host bodies.

How a man looks, how his body functions – all is engrained in his DNA codes. Any mutation in any DNA code can affect the function that the code controls. For instance, cancer of the throat, breast, lungs, or any other part happens due to mutation of DNA controlling growth of cells. Owing to the mutation, cells in the affected tissues divide and grow abnormally, thereby causing cancer.

Retrovirus is a form of virus that creates DNA out of RNA and integrates this DNA into its host genes. Basically, retroviruses are a specialised class of virus that can modify the genetic structure of host genes. The most well-known retrovirus is HIV (Human Immunodeficiency Virus) which corrupts the genetic code of cells involved in the immune system, thereby leading to Acquired Immune Deficiency Syndrome (AIDS).

Retrovirus is the only scientific explanation to the transformation that had resulted in Yuckman. My guess is that the man who is now Yuckman was constantly exposed to muck, and probably engaged in coprophagia. Faecal matter is factory-house of many types of bacteria and fungi. Regular intake of faecal matter could lead to various diseases. The body would naturally try to adapt to the constant flow of toxin and bacterial matter. Somehow, and this is not improbable or unheard of, the concoction of faecal matter and toxins in his stomach mutated some benign viruses in his stomach into retrovirus. The resulting retrovirus had codes to endure and adjust to the habit of coprophagia. The retrovirus installed these codes in different specialised tissues of the man. This transformed the man into Yuckman, a creature whose metabolism runs efficiently and successfully on wastes.

Not only did the retrovirus cause Yuckman's anatomy to change, it also mutated few of the many bacteria that had come to live inside his body because of his shit-eating habits. Certain bacteria are responsible for fermentation of biodegradable wastes (as happens in any biogas plant). After Yuckman's stomach mutated into a functional biogas plant, few bacteria also mutated under the influence of retrovirus to function as fermentation agents. These bacteria developed a symbiotic relation with the mutated digestive system.

I write a small report detailing my theory on Yuckman and send it to the committee. I request for a discussion on my report in the next committee meeting.

I get a call from one Colonel Saket Giri a day after I submit my report. He says that he wants to meet me to discuss my report. *But wasn't the report confidential?* He chooses to ignore my remark and says coldly that his men are on the way to my home. They will escort me to his office at the Directorate of Military Intelligence, City unit.

The man calling himself Colonel Saket Giri hangs up before I could ask anything. As soon as he hangs up, someone knocks at my door. I open the door to find two well-built men in black uniforms. One is tall and lean. The other is stout and looks mean.

"We have been sent by Colonel Giri to escort you to his office," the tall person explains, looking bored.

"Let me change. You did not give me enough time's notice," I object.

"That's not our problem. We have been asked to escort you to the office," says the stout one.

"We only follow orders," the tall one adds.

This pisses me. After all, I have not committed any crime. I am ready to help any officer in any way, but this is not the way to ask for help.

"What if I decide not to come?" I ask.

"That's your problem. We are here to escort you to our operations office. We shall do our duty notwithstanding anything," the stout one says. They do not give me time to change into pants, perhaps just to demonstrate that they mean what they just said. I am hushed away in the dhoti I am wearing.

Tall-and-lean and Stout-and-mean take me to a non-descript shop house in a busy market place. I do not remember ever seeing any MI office in the area. They open the shutters of the shop, take me in, and close the shutters behind them. Then one of them operates a lever and stairs going somewhere underground appear.

They look at me haughtily, perhaps trying to read surprise in me. I am not ready to oblige them. "Is it necessary to make a secret chamber for military intelligence gathering in *this* city?" I ask sarcastically. "This is neither Srinagar nor Kohima."

Both feel piqued by my comment.

We go down the stairs and reach a state-of-the-art underground office containing multiple chambers. I am impressed. The government must have made a good investment in preparing this safe house.

I am taken to Colonel Saket Giri's chamber. He is tall and fair, square-jawed with a toned face, in his mid-thirties; he sits in his chamber in formal attire. No uniform. After exchanging formalities, he asks the escorts to leave and directly comes to the point.

"Brother, I have gone through the report you plan to present to the committee formed for investigating Yuckman appearances. There is nothing new about the report. That Yuckman can be a mutant is already a theory floating around. What's remarkable about the report is your explanation of how this person's metabolism works. Somehow this makes your report sound logical and convincing."

"Also the analysis of DNA tests on Yuckman, which kind of proves the mutant theory," I wonder aloud.

Giri looks at me raptly. "Yes brother, yes. Look, we have shredded the copy of the report you had submitted to the fucking committee. No one other than the chairman has seen it. You should *not* circulate any further copies. You see, the fucking media is keeping a close watch on proceedings of your committee. If they lay their fucking hands on something like this, they may create problems for us, you know..."

"No, I do not know. I do not understand anything of what you are saying. And who are you to instruct me not to present a report I have written for the committee to its members?" I retort sharply.

"My mistake," Giri says, betraying a snoot that seems to say he does not ever consider himself mistaken. "I must explain the context to you. Let's start with...umm...err... comics. Superhero comics. We do not have much superhero nonsense in India. But superheroes are popular in western cultures. The gist about every superhero fiction is that there is a stupid *hero* with superhuman powers. Being the hero, he is benevolent and *protects* people from villains. Some of these villains have superhuman powers, while others do not.

"And how do they get their superhuman powers? Most explanations revolve around extrinsic factors – either they get bitten by a mutant bug or they get exposed to radioactivity etcetera etcetera. Superman is an exception to this. He is an alien. But then, Superman is also boring. He is invincible: strong as steel, flies, and has heightened senses. In one of the comics, he even changes the rotational speed of the earth. In short, the fucker is not a man. He does not have flaws. He does not have limitations. Superman is a fucking alien, not a 'super man'.

"Batman? Batman is not a superhero. He is just a masked vigilante. Remove Superman and Thor – who is a god – and we have superhero stories where the protagonist is a *human* with superhuman strengths. An inherent flaw that these stories suffer from is that invariably the protagonist is a 'good' man. He follows a strong moral code. He is ready to risk his life to protect people. He is a saviour. Tell me brother, would you obsess yourself with protecting stupid assholes if you get Spiderman's powers? May be you will. I am not negating the possibility of you being fucking *good*. But an overwhelmingly high probability remains that you will not. That's human nature. People are all selfish and brutish. Give a man superpowers and he won't even care for the mother's cunt he came out of. We do not disclose our true nature because of fear of punishment. If you get some secret power, the reality is you will misuse it to make money and pussy.

"This explains Yuckman: a real-life superhuman who could not handle the fact that he has suddenly got lethal powers. His powers have overwhelmed him. More importantly, he is a simpleton. Nothing but an idiot. His needs are purely on a basic level: money and honey. He has no agenda: good or evil. You may argue he is evil because he kills randomly. No. I cannot say why he fucking kills people at random, but I can say with reasonable definiteness that he does not have any greater design behind it. He is a dog, and I am quoting Joker from the Batman movies here, he is a dog chasing a car. He wouldn't know what to do with one if he caught up.

"Now, Yuckman, this bastard is more than just a superhuman. He marks the beginning of the end for human species. His rise from some stinking gutter foretells the rise of a new dominant species to take over from us humans.

"Before I explain why Yuckman is important, let me tell you what future is for the human race minus the Yuckman angle. Of course this is my theory on what the future of our species is.

"How do animals normally evolve? By adaptation, of course. An animal which can adapt to its surroundings survives. Others do not. Dinosaurs got screwed because their progeny could not survive changing climate conditions. Woolly mammoths went extinct at the time of the last glacial retreat; modern elephants, smart cunts, adapted and survived. Scientists give us myriad such examples. The point is that climate change is fucking serious.

"The history of evolution is the history of climate change. But then climate changes have been happening mostly due to natural causes, such as changes in sunspots, volcanic activity, plate tectonics, etc. But in recent times – by recent times I mean last 300-400 years, which is recent in the chronology of the earth's history – climate change has been happening because of human-induced reasons.

"This brings us to global warming. Man must produce; man must consume. To top it man is fucking and reproducing at a rapid rate – our species is no better than bovines – which means greater stress on the resources at our disposal and a greater generation of waste. As a result, ecology does not just change, it degrades. Global warming is a bitch.

"You take the case of this city. *Citizens* of the City are not aware of the *denizens* of the dark and the deploring underbelly that lies hidden behind the high-rises, shine and splendour of the City. Inside the City, grand shopping malls and dirty slums co-exist. 'Mall environment' is different from 'slum environment'. Two different ecologies – sharply at contrast with each other – coexist in the City. 'Mall environment' is supplied with potable water, sanitised bathrooms, and air-conditioned rooms. Mall-kids move around in AC cars. People who can afford to stay in the mall environment are affluent people. They are the ones who have the ability to *consume*. If the season is hot, they get air-conditioning. If the season is cold, they use room heating systems. The by-product of their consumption is waste which has to be disposed somewhere. Where? Since the mall environment has no use for wastes, wastes are dumped in the slum environment. In short, the rich are subsidised by the poor.

"Slum environment – this is where water and air carry diseases. People living in the slum environment are the ones who experience extremes of conditions. Slum environment is the place where you get to see natural selection in open demonstration. There are myriad reasons not to survive the decayed ecosystem. Weak children mostly die at childbirth. The scene here is not like the mall environment where the weak are survived in incubators and assisted by numerous nurses and doctors. Those who are weak but have miraculously survived childhood in the slum environment fade away within years. But those who survive have managed to *adapt*. Their after-generations shall have stronger ability to survive and interact with polluted environs.

"Now there is something about these slum-rats that affluent people are missing out on. The rich are not sufficiently exposed to bad environment. My son gets loose motions whenever he consumes street food. He only drinks bottled water; he catches a fever if he drinks normal water. But kids of the street have been surviving quite well after eating street food and drinking tap water.

"As a result, we have two different sets of human species evolving in different motherfucking directions. Slum rats either perish by sickness and malnutrition or develop adaptive genes to take their lineage forward. Mall kids breed in artificial, controlled climate and so do not develop adaptive genes. In say two hundred or three hundred years from now, global warming will lead to drastically different climatic challenges than the present. There will be so much waste that there will be nothing but waste. Natural resources will decline. Energy resources will decline. The challenge before motherfucker humans will be, a) to survive such an eco-system and, b) to generate energy and other resources from mass of wastes. At that time we will see that the sisterfucker slum rats have evolved into a new species; a new species that can survive extremely degraded ecosystem. This new species will not only survive degraded conditions, it will have the ability to sustain over wastes.

"I call this species *Homo Shitens* because shit is symbolic of wastes. Human species will face mass extinction sometime between now and then. Of course, some scientists and zoologists of the *Homo Shitens* species will conserve specimens of our species in laboratories and zoos (with artificially controlled climate). For all practical purposes, humans will give way to their successor, thanks to capitalistic pursuits and conspicuous consumption.

"This is my theory on the future of civilization. I have a firm belief that our successor species will rise much faster than we succeeded those fucker *Homo Erectus*. Now we come to the point: why is that bastard Yuckman so important? You see brother, evolution usually happens by adaptation. But there are other ways of evolution, such as mutation and random shift. By mutation, this Yuckman has already acquired the skills to survive extreme environs and extract energy from wastes. The new species *may* have arrived before its time."

Giri takes a gulp of water and putting his hand on his chin, looks distantly at the ceiling. Perhaps he is thinking, or posing like a thinker, or expects me to believe that he is a philosopher of sorts. There are many flaws in his theory. Giri is not a man of science, evidently. His knowledge of evolution is skin-deep, reason why he could afford to propound such a simplistic theory. And I cannot but resist the need to point out mistakes.

"Your theory of evolution, Mr Giri, only shows that you do not understand evolution in its entirety," I say. Giri is piqued.

"Evolution is a complex process," I continue, "And it is simply impossible to predict where it leads. You said that pollution is bringing about changes in our immediate environment, which will naturally lead to adaptive changes in future generations. I agree with you on this. One of the most cited examples on adaptation is that of moths in the face of industrial pollution. A species of moths called *Biston betularia* is found in England. Before the industrial revolution, these moths were of a light pepper colour. This helped moths camouflage easily with surrounding trees. During the industrial revolution, pollution caused trees in the industrial areas to become darker. A few dark coloured offspring of normal moths had better chances of survival in the industrial areas because they could easily camouflage with darker trees. Slowly dark moths dominated over the light moths in polluted areas. Within a span of hundred years from the time the dark colour moths were first detected, it was found that ninety percent of moths in polluted areas were dark in colour. However, in unpolluted areas the light colour form was still common.

"The case with humans is vastly different. Humans are much more complex beings than moths. Unlike in moths, the adaptive process happens in humans in stages. Significant changes in the structure of humans can only happen by a cumulative adaptive process; and it will take ages. It is very improbable that humans will give way to another species in just two hundred or three hundred years.

"I also have reservations about your theory that the poor have a better chance at adaptation than the rich. You see, the most prominent difference between us humans and our ape ancestors is not legs or hands; it is the brain. Humans have a complex brain structure; most prominent feature of evolution in the case of Homo sapiens remains the brain. Coming back to your thesis of the rich and the poor evolving in different directions, remember that poor people do not get an enriched environment. Many poor children suffer from malnutrition which directly affects their mental ability. Rich kids, on the other hand, get good nutritious food and clean air.

"Secondly, the brain develops in kids when they are supplied with rich, stimulating environment. Take the case of my grandson. I am amazed at how fast he learns. He is just five years old now and he can search for facts on Google; he can browse through pictures and select TV channels. His mother makes him learn poems and stories we had learnt when we were nine or ten years old. It is because of exposure. Think about an average fourteen-year-old teen now. He is much different from how you were when you were fourteen. A fourteen-year-old teen today is faced with an information overload you had never experienced in your times. The school syllabus is becoming more and more complex; then there is the pressure of performing well in entrance examinations. They also have to excel in extra-curricular activities. My point is that affluent kids have better development of mental faculties. This way they have a better chance at survival than poor kids.

"And then there is the obvious edge your mall kids have over your slum rats. Since their parents are rich, they get better life chances: which means better chances at survival and reproduction.

"I do not mean to say that your theory is not plausible. It is. Indeed, poor people have greater ability to tolerate extremes of temperature. But it is also possible that something else happens. Maybe man will give way to two, not one, species: one intelligent but physically weak and another strong but dumb. They will find a way to co-exist.

"Theory of evolution by natural selection helps us explain all that has happened; but it cannot foretell us what is to happen. This is because natural selection does not follow any logic or design. It happens by trial and error. Let us say a genetic error happens when a baby is born and he grows to become a bald man. A bald head is neither adaptive nor mal-adaptive. So he survives and reproduces like any other man. But say the genetic error makes his lung resistant to lead poisoning. This is an adaptive error. He will not only survive but his progeny have a better chance of survival in the face of lead pollution."

"Minus the intricate logic, brother, that's the point I am making. In the face of a strongly polluted ecosystem and depleting resources, a new species has to come in order to survive," Giri says.

"Or may be evolution cannot keep up with rapidly depleting environment and we will go extinct. Just like woolly mammoths or dinosaurs. That's why climate change has become such a pressing cross-national issue these days," I retort. "But that is not the issue here. The issue is that of Yuckman. You are very much right; he is a mutant. Most instances of mutation are mal-adaptive in nature. Many victims of Bhopal gas tragedy or of Hiroshima nuclear bomb explosion are mutants. They have developed hereditary defects. Their mutations have been mal-adaptive in nature. But Yuckman's mutation is adaptive."

Giri just looks at me without expression. It appears to me he does not like being corrected.

"Okay," I say after a moment. "You still have not explained to me why all this is confidential. We do realise all that is written in my report is little more than conjecture. Many other people around may float such theories. Don't you think so?"

"The reason we do not want your report in the committee is because we are feeding all sorts of wrong news to the public and press through the committee. Pressmen are bastards. We do not want them creating nuisance around. We inject incorrect and often contradictory facts about Yuckman through the committee. This way people are not sure about what is right and what is wrong.

"When a common man proposes a theory X to explain Yuckman, we propose theory Y and theory Z and incorrect facts to substantiate these theories to contradict theory X. But we have to show the public that a committee of experts is working on revealing Yuckman. That's why we have frequent committee meetings; but such meetings do not involve anything serious. All meetings are orchestrated. The chairman of the committee, that arse Sinha, is a NTRO man. He has intentionally started an ego issue with the..."

"What is NTRO?" I interrupt.

It does not occur to me that these military types do not like to be interrupted.

"I shall ignore the impropriety of your interruption this time. NTRO is National Technical Research Organisation. It's an elite surveillance, interception and investigation wing of prime minister's office. NTRO is the lead agency investigating into the Yuckman issue. So I was saying that Dr Sinha is intentionally picking up issues with the police commissioner. The press is getting meaty bites; so their focus has shifted from the real issue. Now brother, you may speak."

"From what I understand, you have some designs about how to deal with Yuckman. And you want to keep all this undercover. Right?"

"Not me. The government has plans for the bastard. Trust me, we are lucky that a man from our country has mutated into Yuckman. There are many other third world countries with horrid settlements and living conditions for citizens at the bottom – there is Brazil with some of the largest slums in the world to boast about, then there are Argentina, Pakistan, Iran, Bangladesh, half of Africa, even China. But our motherland has been chosen by destiny as an incubator of Yuckman. Yuckman is our national property.

"Many countries are getting curious about Yuckman. Pricks in American and Japanese embassies have started asking prying questions. You know why they are interested? Yuckman's anatomy has many mysteries, the exact nature of which we can only ascertain when we apprehend and examine him.

"Yet another party showing much interest in Yuckman is a group of creationists. Creationists are ideologues who denounce Darwin's theory of evolution as anti-Christ. They claim that all living beings were created by intelligent design of a divine force. They are an international group propagating a counter-theory that Darwin's theory of natural selection is unscientific and wrong. I have come to know from reliable sources that many creationists from all over the country and outside have come to the city scavenging for Yuckman. They see Yuckman as a threat to their theory of living beings. In fact, I am trying to track down a Father Paulo Sodano who has let loose a network of creationists, posing as tourists, religious leaders and even homeless beggars, to track down Yuckman."

"I wonder why you would reveal all this to me... that too when all this information is supposed to be classified," I state.

"Our government works in funny ways," Giri says and pouts. "The defence minister feels that the action team formed to deal with Yuckman does not have a civilian," he continues after pausing for a breath. "The action team is led by NTRO personnel and has representatives of the Intelligence Bureau (IB), the Military Intelligence (MI), the Council of Scientific and Industrial Research (CSIR) and the Defence Research & Development Organisation (DRDO). We also have representatives from the External Affairs Ministry and office of Chief Scientific Advisor to PM in the team. The team is loaded with servicemen and government scientists. The minister feels that the team should have a representative from the common public. We have been searching for someone who fits the criteria and at the same time could contribute to the team. When some team members read your report, they asked me to do a background check on you. You are a retired academic from an IIT with sound exposure of biochemistry.

There is nothing in your past record that would suggest doubts about your integrity. So, welcome to the team."

"You have a funny way of welcoming new members to your team. Your men literally dragged me out of my house," I say. (I am secretly elated. If they can give luxurious indulgences to members of the fake committee, there must be lot more in store.)

"Oh those two...I have nicknamed them Changu and Mangu. I had asked the dickheads to escort you with all due respect. May be they were cracking a practical joke at your expense. Now coming to our team, you have to keep your involvement in it confidential. All activities of the action team are privileged. You rat us out, we tear your ass apart. We will be apprehending Yuckman soon. As soon as he arrives at our lab, you have to consistently engage with all specialists and involve yourself with the proceedings that will follow. If you disagree with any decision or have reservations about any proposal in the lab, you talk to me. I am the defence minister's stud in the lab."

"I will be glad to help in any way possible. But tell me, how are you so confident about being able to apprehend him soon? I have read all reports on Yuckman sightings. It seems police are helpless because he is agile and can vanish into a sewer or swamp. No tactics used by the police in their pursuit could help them."

"There is a reason behind that," Giri explains. "Initially the local police was dumb-founded when they faced the Yuckman scare. However, later they did understand how to tackle him. After all he is just a human. Gunshots have the potential of damaging his body parts. So it is that simple: get some sharp shooters on the job and keep a rapid action team on its toes. But this is what worried us. We want Yuckman in our possession in one piece. Unhurt. Local police have been strictly instructed not to engage with Yuckman in any way and immediately inform us whenever they get any information about him. Our field personnel are from IB. They will engage with Yuckman only if they can apprehend him without causing any damage."

"By doing that you are basically putting the common man's life at risk."

"There always is some collateral damage, brother. The common man is anyway a fucker. Contributes nothing to the country and keeps fucking to increase the nation's population. Now let's not go into that. It's a policy decision taken by the steering committee of the team."

"I still do not understand how you will catch Yuckman. With his powers of agility and ability to vanish into sewers, he remains elusive."

"We know where he is. On analysing the City's contours, we found a huge island of garbage in one corner of the City. I call it 'island' because it's a patch of land surrounded by open gutters on all sides. Most of the garbage of the City is offloaded in this patch. In its own way, it is a beautiful place... You will find nothing but heaps of garbage in Garbage Island. It is also an extremely smelly and intolerable area. Yet, to my surprise, there is a small slum of illegal Bangladeshi bastards inside Garbage Island. One of our investigating officers went there undercover and made some enquiries. It seems a curious creature has been cited there many times in the last few weeks...often found rummaging through garbage. Guess what, the description matches that of Yuckman. Few arses in the slum could guess that the creature is Yuckman. Yet none of them illegal bastards reported to the police because, after all, they are illegal immigrants."

Changu and Mangu (I am still confused which one is who) escort me back to my house after my meeting with Giri ends. They admit, rather reluctantly, that they have been assigned to me and will be available at my disposal till further orders. I am overwhelmed by the benefits of feasting on curiosity and scare of government and community. Thank you, whoever you are, Filthy Fiend...

Garbage Island

Durugi is the goddess of harmony. Trees, herbs, animals, insects, birds, and humans live at peace with each other and nature because of her. In a way, she is the mother goddess. She is full of kindness and tender love. Sibu's mother Mali used to say that Dharama may be powerful but Durugi is special. This is because she has a special power Dharama does not possess: the power of creation.

"Kind that Durugi is, she made every woman special. She gave women the power to create: to give birth. Yet women have been subjugated and discriminated against in the so-called civilised society. Female gender is the prime casualty in a caste-based society. Women are ill-treated and forced into restrictions. It is just like the way company people and builders molest Durugi by uprooting forests. Civilised men are known by the way they treat women. Look at the irony: these men of caste society claim to be more civilised than us Tikna folk! We Tikna folk are part and parcel of Durugi's nature. We revere Durugi. That's why you will find respect in our men for women. Sibu, my moon, never misbehave with women," Mali had said.

Lying all alone in a heap of garbage in a moon-lit night, Sibu was overwhelmed by memories of his mother. Her life had been full of sorrow. With dozens of children and two husbands, she never really had time to relax and enjoy. She would do her best to satiate the kids' appetite; although she herself lived on an empty stomach many times. She would dare pick up fights with both alcoholic husbands only for her children. She was the only earning member of both the families. Yet she was pushed around, kicked around. She got no love, no respect. What respect did her husbands give her? They were Tiknas, after all.

Yellow coloured tears rolled down Sibu's eyes. His mother had remained perpetually hungry. She grew consistently weak with starvation. She was horribly weak and sick in her last days, mainly because of starvation. Even then, all she was worried about was her children. What happened to his siblings? Where are they? Sibu wondered.

Sibu was stuck with feelings of guilt. The Great God Dharama had given him special powers and he had used them to kidnap and rape women. He had found violence on women erotic. He seemed to enjoy it. But all this time he did not realise how painful it must have been for his victims. If his mother were alive, she would have held him in contempt: her little prince had turned out to be a savage offender.

Sibu had thrown acidic excretion from his body on the last woman he had kidnapped. The very thought of the way she wriggled in pain brought jitters in him. How had he changed so much so suddenly? Or was he just like this all along? It appeared to him that the transformation not only turned his looks ugly, but also his character.

Sibu resolved never to force himself on any woman. But then, how would he fill this emptiness inside him? Of late he has been feeling lonelier than ever. Even when he had come to the City and did not know any language other than his native Tikna tongue, he did not feel this lonely. He had to necessarily avoid people because of his unusual situation.

Sibu had tried to communicate with some people in Garbage Island. This was a place close to his heart and he always came over to Garbage Island after few days of wandering across the City. He had thought that the people of Garbage Island would, at least, accept him given that they have comfortably assimilated into the environs of Garbage Island. But when he approached a few men sitting by the lone pan shop in Garbage Island, they panicked and threw stones at him.

He could have retaliated. But he did not have the heart to do so. They were his neighbours. Like him, they were people of filth and crap. He took two giant leaps and vanished into a heap of garbage.

Later Sibu befriended a sixteen-year-old orphan Ali. Ali made a living by scavenging for plastic bags through the great heaps of waste in Garbage Island. Sibu had confronted him while he was collecting odd scraps from garbage. Ali did not panic on seeing him. Sibu offered him some money he had robbed during his shopping mall raids. Ali eagerly accepted the money.

Ali was just about four-and-a-half feet in height. He was emaciated and dirt-coloured. Even his hair was dry and brown. He wore a torn t-shirt and black shorts, clothes that were probably never washed. He could camouflage well with the refuse of Garbage Island; and indeed he did. Sibu would give him some money every time they met. In return, all Ali had to do was give him company. Sibu knew that Ali hardly understood his blabbers, but the fact that a human listened to him was comforting.

Ali appeared at this moment and leaned over Sibu, displaying an innocent smile. It was as if he had sensed Sibu's loneliness.

"What are you thinking about Sibu?" Ali asked.

"Actually about you, little friend," Sibu said, enthused.

"Look what I have got for you," Ali said and showed him a brown latex overcoat. "You will look good in it. It will be your uniform. Look, I have also salvaged goggles and a brown hat for you. You should wear these like other superheroes."

"What heroes?" Sibu asked, examining the red coloured goggles with interest.

"Superheroes. People who are abnormal but can use their special talents to create brands. This world is all about marketing. It's not like your simple jungle village. Here you are famous if you can sell yourself to people. To sell yourself to people, you need to develop your brand value. You need to look smart. And do some things, things like...like save some kids or women from bad men. Then ensure that the news gets good media coverage. That way you will increase your worth in society. You are despised because you are infamous. You are infamous because you are despised. You need to change that," Ali said.

Sibu did not understand what Ali said, yet dutifully nodded. "Tell me Ali, where do you learn all these hi-fi ideas?"

"I roam around and meet people, so I know a lot. Listen, I also have a pair of gloves and hard shoes that will be just fine for you. Try them on. I think if you wear all these things I give you, people will not be able to recognise you. And here," Ali took out a perfume bottle, "this is to hide the smell. Although I doubt any perfume could suppress your repugnant stink, this can help subdue it. Put on the overcoat and the accessories and try to mix up with people of the slum. See if you can blend in. Got me?"

Sibu nodded.

"Now now, I must get going. I have some work at the slum. Farewell," Ali said and sprinted away.

Sibu heeded Ali's advice and drifted through the inhabited areas of Garbage Island wearing the costume Ali had given him. At first he had apprehensions that people would notice him. They did notice him; a man walking around in an oversized coat, cowboy hat and red goggles naturally drew their attention. But they could not guess that this was the delinquent Yuckman. Curious onlookers gossiped about his purpose of visit to Garbage Island. Few suspiciously speculated that he might be an undercover police officer. After a few days, however, they lost interest.

One evening Sibu overheard two old men talking animatedly at the pan shop about a dance troupe. The dance troupe had camped in Garbage Island and had decided to perform two shows daily. It was a first for Garbage Island. No circus, no opera, no dance troupe had ever performed in Garbage Island before. It was a colony of poor, illegal Bangladeshi immigrants. What money could they shell out for an entertainment programme? Yet this year, a dance troupe had decided to perform in the otherwise unmelodic airs of Garbage Island.

"Guess what?" said a mullah with a long, white beard and pan-stained teeth to another old man, "Malvika Gadnayak is going to perform in tonight's show."

"Who is Malvika Gadnayak?" asked the other old man curiously, "her name sounds so sweet."

"I don't know. But I have overheard my nephew saying she is this luscious, curvaceous girl from the City people go mad about. As she dances, her gyrating hips make you perspire even in the height of winter. When she whirls her little bum and throws her bosoms around, your heart will go cold with desire even in the hottest of months," explained the mullah. "Let's attend tonight's show. It's been a long time since we had some action. Understand what I mean...eh? Heyn...heyn...heyn."

"Is she really that good, this Malvika Gadnayak? Has your nephew seen her perform?" asked the other old man.

"No, no. He has heard from a friend. But why worry about it when you will see her live, in flesh, tonight! Do not worry about tickets...the shows are open for all. Heyn...heyn... heyn..." exclaimed the mullah and laughed like a hyena.

Sibu overheard the mullah speak of the maiden he had overheard his nephew speak of. Although he had resolved to control his cravings, Sibu got curious about this Malvika Gadnayak. Sibu decided he would attend the dance show as well. It had been a long time since he had had some action...

The dance troupe's performance that evening had a heavy turnout. Almost the whole of Garbage Island had turned up to watch the show. The evening's programme started with an anchor making poor jokes. Then there was a group dance on a patriotic theme. It was ironic since the audience were all illegal Bangladeshi immigrants. This was followed by a solo recitation of a devotional song.

Just when the audience was getting bored, the anchor returned and cracked another joke. The audience resented his joke with shots of peanuts, vegetables and bottles.

"Keep patience my friends...because to come in our midst, to come in our midst, is none other than the queen of beauty, the rare shard of the moon, Maaal-vika Gaddnayak. Maaal-vika Gaddnayak!" the anchor shouted into his mike, while trying to escape the jet of junk food being hurled at him. "Only for your entertainment, brothers and sisters, aged and the underage, lewds and innocents, for the first time in the history of Garbage Island, comes in our midst: Malvika Gadnayakk. Malvika Gadnayakk!"

The anchor faded away as the stage darkened. Then a red beam appeared and focussed on a pair of heaving breasts. Music from a popular Bollywood song started playing. The beam vanished and a yellow beam appeared. It focussed on the back of a woman, while she gyrated to the tunes of the Bollywood song. The audience cried out in anticipation and jubilation. Whistles were blown from all corners of the arena.

This scene was followed by lights from all corners of the podium and the audience got its first glimpse of the Queen of Beauty, Malvika Gadnayak. She was petite – about five-feet-two in height – and wheatish; her breasts were huge and her bottom was enormous. She was wearing a short, colourfully embroidered skirt and a matching blouse. A part of her fleshy belly sprouted out of the skirt occasionally as she danced. She was indulgently dancing to the craving eyes of her audience and to the tunes of a cheesy song.

Paste my photo... Ho paste my photo
To your chest with fevicol
With fevicol haye, with fevicol
Paste my photo... Ho paste my photo
To your chest with fevicol
With fevicol haye, with fevicol

Since when I am ready and all
Woo me with a missed call

Hmm... make love today with this fairy's daughter
Make love today with this fairy's daughter
You will forget all morals with a quarter

Those who drink me will get the real pleasure of living
I am the kind of thing that gets you high on water
I m a roasted...
Haye I am a roasted chicken
Gulp me down with alcohol
With alcohol haye, with alcohol
Paste my photo to your chest
With fevicol haye, with fevicol

Among the lascivious men in the audience following each and every move of her body was an odd man in cowboy hat and long brown overcoat. It was Sibu. Like the others, he was captivated by this beautiful creature, Malvika Gadnayak. Sibu had never seen any other woman as skilful a dancer as her.

The song continued:

My Gypsy is ready with siren et al
Run it away with petrol
With petrol haye, with petrol
Paste my photo! Ho paste my photo
To your chest with fevicol
With fevi fevicol haye, with fevicol

Few unruly men from the audience jumped over the security ring onto the makeshift stage and started dancing around Malvika Gadnayak. They sang:

We will make love to you, o baby doll
Woo you with a missed call
With bat ball, haye with cinema hall

Oh sex siren and symbol
We will stick into your goal
Our cannonball with fevicol
With fevicol haye, with fevicol...

Bouncers crept up to the stage to control the unruly mass. After few minutes of jostling and a heated conversation, the show organisers managed to send the trespassers back to the audience arena. However, Malvika Gadnayak was gone by then.

Sibu wanted this woman – Malvika Gadnayak. An inner voice reminded him of the resolution he had made not to force himself on any woman. And now here he was thinking about yet another girl. Sibu reasoned that he could make an exception. Just one exception: this woman was worth breaking a resolution to Goddess Durugi. Sibu had finalised his plans to abduct Malvika Gadnayak by the time the crowd dispersed at the dance festival.

Creationists

One fine day a white man comes knocking at my door. He is blonde, has hazel eyes, and wears a long, black cassock. A cross hangs by a silver chain around his neck. Evidently he is a Catholic priest, but why is he here to visit me? He introduces himself as Father Paulo Sodano from Italy and wants to come in for a small chat.

His name sounds familiar, but I cannot place it. He is a stranger, so I hesitate to invite him in. He senses my hesitation and assures me he won't be taking much of my time. I recall the context in which I had heard his name only after I invite him in, and instantly regret having done so. Giri had mentioned Paulo Sodano as a creationist who had come to India after reading about Yuckman sightings in the papers.

"I shall be frank with you about my visit, professor," Father Sodano says. "I have been sent by the Vatican to investigate into the curious incidents surrounding this person the Indian media calls Yuckman."

"Why have you come to me?" I ask tentatively.

"For an intellectual conversation, professor. You are a member of the Mayor's committee to enquire into Yuckman. I am told that you are wise and well read."

There is a brief silence in which we size each other up.

"So professor, I will start with a personal question. Are you a man of God?" Sodano asks.

"I pray. I respect God. But if you are asking me if I am religious..."

"No," he interrupts, "I am asking you if you have faith in God. Whether you have surrendered yourself to God? Do you acknowledge that everything that was, is, and will be, is what God plans?"

"Well, if you put it that way, I do not subscribe to blind faith. I do question things, but it is not just about God. I question everything...that's scientific temper. I am a man of science."

"I too am a man of science, professor," Sodano says. "I am a doctorate in particle physics from Carnegie Melon University. I value scientific discovery. I believe science drives our civilisation forward. Technology has made our lives better. But this does not mean I am not a man of God. Science is trying to help us understand the way things work. The more I understand about how things work, the more is my conviction in God. Think about it – that table, this chair, your spectacles – they are all made up of compounds. The compounds are made up of elements. Each element has a different atomic structure. Atoms in themselves are so complex, there are tomes on each sub-atomic particle...on electrons, protons, neutrons, quarks, leptons, bosons. Think about how intricately these sub-atomic particles interact, how magnificently atoms interact. Science has helped me understand the beauty behind things. Science has convinced me that such intricate design – design that we still research in myriad labs – could not have happened by chance. This is God's design."

"If I may be frank, the Church is not very comfortable embracing science. The Church has opposed genetic research, test tube babies, also the large Hadron Collider that tries to understand sub-atomic particles."

"Those in the Church who do are fools. They are the ones diseased with blind belief. I have been vocal in the Vatican about my views. My view is that science is a tool for us to understand and appreciate the complex and marvellous world, and universe, created by God. No other force could have possibly brought together such diverse ideas, mechanisms and processes that our world is."

"I want to correct myself." I see that the priest is playing with words, "I am not a man of science as you put it. I am a man of *objectivity*. I am open to different points of view, but when I have to come to a conclusion, I go by *facts* and *logic*."

Sodano smiles slyly, "You are a man of *objectivity*, professor. Then I am afraid you are also diseased with blind faith. Objectivity is an oxymoron. Let me explain how in three steps:

"A. In order to be objective, you negate all that is surreal.

"B. You have not yet objectively established that what you consider surreal is not real.

"C. Hence you make a bias when you are objective.

"Let me illustrate this with an example. The Lord, Jesus Christ, was born to Virgin Mary and God. Do you believe in virgin births?"

"Virgin births do happen and it is called parthenogenesis," I say. "Parthenogenesis has been observed in simpler creatures, but impossible in vertebrates. Many species of ants, for example, reproduce by themselves. There is a species of whiptail lizards in which there is no male. All members of this species are females. Yet, this particular species of whiptail lizards, if I remember well, does not procreate without sexual intercourse. Two females of the species engage in intercourse, whereby they exchange each other's sperm. Technically the lizards do not demonstrate parthenogenesis; they are lesbian lizards.

"The process of conception in vertebrates is complex and cannot happen without a male. Animals higher in the evolutionary ladder follow definitive steps to reproduce; steps that need a male's sperm to trigger the mechanism..."

"Pardon me for interrupting you here, professor," Sodano says, "It appears you are not abreast with recent research and findings on the subject. What you say is what *men of objectivity* used to say before virgin birth in higher animals was detected. You still maintain the same stand because you are not aware of factual evidences that have been recently documented. As recent as on the fourteenth of December, 2001, an adult bonnet-head shark gave birth to a live pup at the Henry Doorly zoo in Nebraska. The shark had been brought into captivity well before she hit puberty, and was kept in a tank in the zoo in the company of other female sharks. She had no contact with any male shark. This aroused the curiosity of the zoo officials who then reported the matter to competent geneticists. Genetic analysis of mother and daughter confirmed that the pup was a virgin-born.

"What's interesting about this incident is that before this bonnet-head shark pup, scientists used to arrogantly ask for 'proof' and were in complete denial of virgin birth in higher animals. Note that this is not the first virgin birth in the history of animals, nor is it a very rare phenomenon. Millions of animals in the wild have given virgin birth. We humans have no means to detect virgin births. We could detect this incidence of virgin birth because the shark was bred in captivity, and because she did not have any contact with any male. Not surprisingly, the next reported virgin shark mother was again found in captivity, seven years later, at the Virginia Aquarium in Virginia Beach.

"Today science has the tools to verify whether a virgin-born carries only genes of her mother. Just thirty years earlier, science did not have the tools to make such genetic analysis. Scientists then, very conveniently, used to shift the onus of proof on the believer. The believer was ridiculed and asked to furnish evidence for his belief. The body of science, as we know even today, is a fraction of the mysteries that abound in this world. Yet, scientists base their objectivity on this limited knowledge base. Scientific temper, professor, has become a religion."

The evangelist is a good orator, and has facts on his fingertips. I interpose, "Virgin birth in a human female is more difficult than in a shark. You see, the eggs a woman carries consist of only single strand of the twenty-three pairs of chromosomes in her other cells. Eggs are formed by *meiosis* and are unfertilised. It is only when a sperm (with another twenty-three single strands of chromosomes) penetrates the egg that the egg fertilises and leads to an embryo."

"Again, professor, there has been at least one reported case of parthenogenesis in humans. A case documented in the October 1995 issue of the journal *Nature Genetics* speaks about a child, FD, who was born by parthenogenesis. Geneticists have reported that an unfertilised egg of FD's mother was activated by some hormonal trigger and started dividing by itself. I must be frank with you professor, I am disappointed with you. This is a landmark development in the field of genetics and you are unaware of it! You are asking questions that the cynical man used to ask half a century ago. You are a cynic of today. You say you are a man of objectivity, but your objectivity is half-a-century old."

I feel piqued.

Sodano continues, "You have not raised the obvious doubt in the birth of Jesus Christ: all reported instances of parthenogenesis report birth of only *daughters*. A virgin mother can only give birth to a daughter. The sex chromosomes in us humans, so also in most other higher animals, come in pairs. The pair in a female is XX and the pair in a male is XY. The manhood of a male is programmed in the genetic codes of Y-chromosome. A cynic, a man of objectivity, having been corrected again and again by scientific detections, would say today that it is *impossible* for a virgin mother to give birth to a son. Virgin Mary could not have been virgin."

"Yes!" the word escapes my mouth, quite involuntarily. I immediately regret it, realising that the evangelist must have come prepared with facts.

"My understanding is that a virgin mother can give birth to a son. It is a rarity, the probability being so thin that any occurrence deserves to be called a miracle. This is how: researchers have found that one in eighty-three thousand people are born with ovotestes (gonads that have both ovary and testes). Please understand, professor, it is a rare condition.

"The egg that ultimately forms the embryo in a normal case has only X sex chromosome. The sperm that penetrates the egg may have X or Y sex chromosome. If it has X chromosome, then the embryo has X-X (one X from each parent) and is a female. If the sperm has Y chromosome, the embryo has X-Y and is a male.

"Male genital organs are programmed in a specific code of Y chromosome called SRY. The SRY code usually is available in Y chromosome; that's why a male child is born only when the father sperm donates a Y chromosome. However, in a mutation during meiosis in the father's sperm, sometimes the SRY gets embedded in the father's X rather than Y. When this sperm (carrying X-chromosome with SRY code) penetrates the egg, the result is a girl with X-X$_{+SRY}$ sex chromosomes. The child is a girl because she has X-X pairing. Yet, because of the SRY code, she also has testes.

"The only other requirement after such hermaphroditism is that on puberty, the girl's ovotestes produce both sperm and egg. If both sperm and egg (of the same mother) travel down the fallopian tube simultaneously, the sperm may fertilise the egg leading to virgin birth: of a male or female child, as the case may be. So a virgin mother can give birth to a son."

I make a face. I am frankly irritated by this irrelevant discussion about the birth of Jesus Christ.

"I understand you are bored, professor. I had to indulge you in this discussion in order to prove a point. The birth of Jesus to Virgin Mary has been questioned by objectivists for centuries now. Such questions have been raised ever since the Renaissance in Europe and the absurdity of Jesus' birth has been growing stronger. You objectivists never proved that virgin birth is impossible. But you put the onus on the believer to prove virgin birth. You have comfortably assumed the impossibility of the virgin birth of Jesus. Is this not blind faith?

"God is a genius. He does not have to correct Himself, because He has the power of foresight. He has built this Universe and has set in motion a series of events. The events follow rules. These are rules made by God. A zebra cannot give birth to a pig. There are restrictions because there is only so much chaos this world can handle. Yet, God has devised ways out of the order of things: science calls these *exceptions*; laymen call these *miracles*."

"Basically what you are driving at is the view of Creationism," I say sarcastically, in order to belittle his persuasive oration.

"No I am not!" he exclaimed. "Creationists are mired by blind faith. Creationism is an ideology, just like objectivity. I am a man of science, professor. I was the top of my class in my MS degree and went on to do a Ph.D. in particle physics, as I have already told you. I am published in many peer reviewed journals. What more do I need to tell you to convince you that I am not a creationist?

"Charles Darwin was a gift of God to mankind. Darwin's theory of evolution is an eye opener for us, and reiterates our faith on the Almighty. Unlike the creationists, I fully subscribe to Darwin's theory of evolution by natural selection. Indeed, it is not a mere theory, rather an established fact. All the variety, all the beauty of flora and fauna have formed by minor errors in reproduction, sustained and pronounced in future generations by adaptation to environment. How simple, yet stellar this mechanism is! Who could have devised such a mechanism but the divine?"

I am flabbergasted. Natural selection happens as a series of accidents. Now this priest says the accidents have been designed. It is preposterous. I keep mum, for I know these evangelists. They won't stop if you start arguing with them.

"Professor, I see you are quite affected by the revelations made by me," he says, pleased with himself. I keep a poker face.

"So, professor, coming to the point...what sequence of unlikely events do you think could have created Yuckman?"

"I am just an honorary member of the Mayor's committee. I really do not know much about Yuckman." I get nervous – if any word slips my mouth and Giri comes to know about it, he will chew me raw.

A sly half-smile forms on Sodano's face, "Alright professor, I will explain it to you. Spiderman, my favourite superhero, is a mutant. He was bitten by a genetically modified spider which gave him special powers. You pick any fiction on mutants. The plot usually involves an external factor that leads to the mutation – be it genetic engineering or exposure to nukes or getting bitten by a bug, there is always an external factor. There are always scientists involved. Do you know why?

"Because the probability of a human being mutating into another creature *naturally* in a single generation is very low. The probability is almost zero. That's why usually an evil scientist is involved in fiction to explain the mutation. But Yuckman, the first mutant superhuman we know of, was not born in a lab. He mutated in the dirty under-alleys of the City. The probability of Yuckman's creation is almost zero. Almost zero but not zero. You and I, we both know the series of unlikely events that must have happened to lead to the mutation that Yuckman is. Jot them down and calculate the probability, professor. In the extreme conditions in which this man mutated, only one in two hundred persons would survive. Of the persons who survive, one in a million would mutate and survive the mutation. The rarity of Yuckman is one in two billion! The total population of this planet is about a billion. Which means this *is* a miracle."

"What are you driving at?" I ask.

"I am trying to say, Yuckman has been created by God for a purpose. God made him special. God does not bless anyone with special-ness unless He has a purpose for the person. Yuckman is God's agent. He has come to guide us through to a new era, a new world order. The Vatican is God's repository in this world. We – I and like-minded servants of the Lord in the Vatican – feel it is our responsibility to nurture this special creation of God till the time he is ready to lead us."

"Okay."

Sodano stands up and comes over to me. He holds my hands in his and asks, "Brother, are you with us in this noble task?"

"I am retired. I do not do noble tasks anymore," I say bluntly.

"Professor, I mean no harm. I only seek to help. Unfortunately the law enforcement officials in this country see me suspiciously. I just need some inside information, and I know you are on the inside. Come on professor, I need some bite. Anything."

"You have come to the wrong person. Now if you will excuse me..."

"I am a resourceful person, professor. Money or whatever interests you will be taken care of."

"No thank you," I say. "I do not engage in anti-national activities. Nor do I maintain social relations with anti-nationals. Please get out of my house."

Sodano looks at me with intense eyes and starts, "But this is for a greater..."

"Please get out of my house or I will call the police."

Lovely Filth. Filthy love

Jagdish Waghmare used to be a busy man. He was the managing partner of M/s. Necrosis Centre for Public Relations & Corporate Communication. He was also personally engaged by many companies as a consultant. But not anymore. These days he could be found brooding over an armchair on the porch of his bungalow all day long.

Till just a year back, Waghmare was an influential figure in the City. He was named among the who's who of the City. His fall came abruptly and with severe consequences. Once it was said that a power party is not complete without Waghmare participating in it. After the fall, socialites shunned his presence. Politicians feared someone may find out their association with Waghmare. Business leaders became wary of all that he knew. It was a severe fall indeed, given that Waghmare's job was to make friends!

Waghmare was a lobbyist. He was a tactician in the complex world of statutes, laws, rules, regulations, and enforcement. And a good one at that. He was 'friends' with many ministers, judges and bureaucrats. Businessmen knew this; hence flocked to him to get their work done. He was nicked 'The One' after they realised he was *the one* man to turn to for solution to any problem. Life was a big party for Waghmare. He would lobby around in the morning and celebrate approved deals with the same people in the evening. Waghmare was all of forty-two years of age at the height of his career. He looked much older, aggravated by thinning hair, fleshy cheeks and a succulent beer belly (from years of socialising).

An important part of being a lobbyist is to be able to provide your beneficiaries with whatever they want. Waghmare used to supply women to many public personalities. Best of the lot, selected personally by Waghmare, were delivered with utmost discretion. Most of these girls were placed in the payroll of his firm Necrosis.

One girl got too attached to a lawmaker. Or maybe the lawmaker got too attached to her. The girl used to accompany him in his tours and parties. The stupid lawmaker had no value for discretion and used to boast her off. People were conscious of them as a couple. She got pregnant. The lawmaker's wife screwed him. He asked the girl to abort the pregnancy. She said no. He offered money. She still said no. She wanted the baby and she wanted him to marry her. He went running to Waghmare with his tail between his legs, "The whore has forgotten her place. Do something; she cannot have that baby. It will be political suicide."

Waghmare used favour and intimidation to influence her to abort the pregnancy. She did but subsequently became depressive. She went to the media with her story. No one dared to write against him – such was Waghmare's clout. Then she committed suicide. She mentioned all the physics, chemistry and biology of her relationship with the lawmaker in a suicide note. Waghmare's Necrosis got a vivid description in the note as a centre for flesh and kink. The police destroyed the suicide note on the spot – such was Waghmare's clout.

Alas! The girl had sent copies of her suicide note to friends and family by email before logging off from the world. Her suicide became the most talked about scandal of that year. Journalists scourged through layers of gossip and rumours to expose Waghmare. Necrosis was projected as a brothel and Waghmare a pimp. Socialites stopped inviting him to parties. Bureaucrats stopped answering his calls. Corporate groups terminated their contracts with Necrosis. For a man whose job was to make friends and influence people, Waghmare was now a pariah.

The sudden turn of events taking Waghmare from 'The One' to just a common man left him unnerved. He turned a recluse (everyone in his circle avoided him anyway) and rarely met anyone.

No wonder Waghmare was extremely reluctant when his niece requested him to grant an appointment to a journalist friend of hers. He did not blame the journalists for his downfall. A hate campaign based on the suicide note had started in the social media and spread like wildfire. When it became big, papers had to publish the scandal. Still he wasn't enthusiastic to meet a journalist. It was only when his niece assured him that the journalist wouldn't bring up the suicide that he agreed.

The journalist called himself M.S. Nethrapal. He looked like he was in his mid-thirties; well-built and well-dressed in a well-ironed black shirt and trousers.

"You don't look like a journalist," Waghmare said, reclining on a sofa.

"Saar, you can tell soo much about people justah by looking at them. I am a bigga fan, saar. Someday I will make it big in carparate communicasons, justah like you," Nethrapal said with a thick Tamil accent.

Waghmare looked at Nethrapal from the corner of his eyes to see whether he was humouring him. Nethrapal seemed to be genuinely pleased to meet him.

"Alright, what do you want?" Waghmare asked, not hiding his displeasure at the meeting.

"Paartnership saar, partnership," Nethrapal said and smiled slyly.

"What partnership?"

"Paartnership in a project that can get us millions and bring you back to the centre of gravitty."

Waghmare looked at Nethrapal warily, "What makes you think I want to be in the *centre of gravity*?"

"Sorry saar, I misunderstood the pleasures you derive from this wretched state you are in," Nethrapal said. "Even so, you must hear outah my proposal."

This time Waghmare could detect sarcasm in his voice.

"I am in no mood to have this conversation," Waghmare said. "I am good the way I am. You are no one to comment on my affairs. Be quick with what you have to say and get lost."

"Saar, you took offence of my words. Please do nat misunderstand me. Let me starta from the beginning. I am a journalist. I may not look like onea, but I am. I freelance for vernacular prints. They want a scoop here, a bite there, they call me. You will nat find my name in any newspaper. I am the information guy. I supply information for money.

"But information can be worth more than the money these paperwallas are willing to pay. Prablem is one must have the ability to extract the money worth information in their ownership. I have information, saar, salid information. But I do nat have the means to encash it. If I go to the newspapers, they will give me peanuts. I want the real price of information.

"Saar, tell me, what has been the most talked about news in media in recent times? Other than the suicide of your Necrosis employee, of course. It has been on tap of the charts, but saar, it was very wrang of her to do this to a respectable citizen like you. She wanted to die, she did. What was the need to malign a great man like you? You were her employer; you gave her bread and butter!

"Anyway, the Necrosis girl's suicide does nat get as much coverage as a man called Eyukkmun. Do you know why? Because the suicide case is a salved case. The news has enough meat and masala to continue hugging headlines for a fortnight or so, but it is already solved. Whereas Eyukkmun is a mystery. No one knows who he is. What he is. What *it* is. On tap of this, he (or it) has created many law and order issues in the City. Public is scared of him. He is being branded as public enemy number one."

"What are you driving at? Even I read the papers, come to the point," Waghmare reproached.

"Saar saar, what I was saying is many vernacular prints have commissioned me to get news about Eyukkmun. Need nat be real news. Need nat be true news. They just need news. Something new about Eyukkmun they can flash. Have you read the interview of a yoga teacher last week in which he says that Eyukkmun took birth from a Tantra priestess's anus, nat from a uterus? I had identified the yoga teacher and taken him to the newsroom.

"I have been selling such news now and then. In the course of my investigation – and here I am coming to the point – in the course of my investigation, I stumbled upon an old friend who is a havildar in the Territorial Army. He said that he had heard from two of his friends, known by their nick Changu and Mangu, that MI – military intelligence – is on the verge of catching Eyukkmun. Through this friend I reached these two jawans, Changu and Mangu. They work as guards for a high ranking officer of MI…"

"Wait, why would MI be interested in Yuckman? He is a law and order issue, right?" Waghmare interposed.

"Exactly saar. This is what I thought when I first heard them. I asked Changu and Mangu to give details. They were not clear why MI wants Eyukkmun – they are havildar rank soldiers and do not get involved in policies. What they had to say is that their officer has been meeting many people in connection with Eyukkmun.

"Changu and Mangu were themselves reluctant to speak to me. They were vague, at most. I greased their hands with some money and they started giving details. Their reporting afficer was posted in another city. He was transferred to the City at a short notice after the Eyukkmun scare became serious. He has assembled a special investigation team to catch Eyukkmun. Again Changu and Mangu were clueless as to why military is interested.

"I too was skeptic about this story. When I grilled them further, Changu conceded that a member of this team is a retired praffessor. Changu and Mangu were asked to attend to his security after he was made a member of the team. He is given round the clock protection. Two gunmen stand guard outside his residence aal the time. Changu and Mangu clock the afternoon shift. Why would the government appoint six soldiers as bodyguards for an insignificant retired teacher?

"I did nat stop here. I dug out the prafessor's credentials. He was one of the first researchers in biochemistry in this country. He is a member of the committee formed by the City mayor to enquire into Eyukkmun. He has never been involved with the army. All these circumstantial evidence do tell us something. May be he is part of a secret hi-profile team to nab Eyukkmun; however, there can be myriad other reasons.

"I had to find out for sure what is happening. Both Changu and Mangu became nervous when I asked them to get me an inlet into MI. MI is a black box saar. It is closely guarded and has many layers of security pratocol. They were not ready to take any chance. Then it occurred to me, why infiltrate into MI if I can keep an eye on the prafessor?

"I cajoled Changu and Mangu to plant bugs inside the prafessor's house. I listened into his conversations. An army afficer has called him regularly. Prablem is they did nat talk much over phone. The afficer used to phone him and ask him to attend this meeting or that meeting at MI office.

"I stuck upon a smart plan. The prafessor always carries a pen when he goes out. He carries the same pen every time he goes out. One day I sneaked into his house while he was sleeping and inserted a micro-bug into the pen.

"The plan did not work. As I found out, MI affice in the City is fitted with an electranic jammer. So my micro-bug could nat communicate any information to me. Frustrated, I had almost given up when, by accident, I chanced upon an old journalist friend who specialises in sting aperations. He had procured an advanced spy device from Dubai which looks like a micro-bug but has a two GB attached cache memory and a strong battery. The electronic circuitry of this device works at a frequency range that jammers usually can't catch.

"I kept listening into the bug planted in this prafessor's house. One day he got a phone call asking him to attend a meeting the next day. I sneaked in that night and planted the special micro-bug in his pen. He went to the meeting and came back. I again sneaked in and removed the micro-bug. I brought it back with me and downloaded its data into my camputer. This is what I found from the interception.

"These people think Eyukkmun is a mutant and will unravel many mysteries that may give Indian gavernment a strategic and military edge. Owing to his mutation, there is a biogas machine inside him and it is different from any other biogas plant. Biogas is produced by anaerobic digestion of organic wastes. Anaerobic digestion is catalysed by certain category of bacteria. This process takes lang time, and the extraction of carbon monoxide and methane gases is not quite efficient. Present biogas technology is not economically a viable alternative to coal for producing energy.

"The process by which Eyukkmun processes wastes to produce gases is much more efficient. CSIR scientists who participate in MI meetings guess that the bacteria in his body have developed some kind of symbiotic relation with his mutant cells. Whatever it is, whoever understands the mechanism becomes the first to develop an alternative to oil and coal as energy source. NTRO, an organisation I had never earlier heard about, is interested in the applications of this mechanism in defence. NTRO believes a new strain of retrovirus has caused the mutation in Eyukkmun. This strain, if introduced in any other person, will give the person similar powers as Eyukkmun's.

"Eyukkmun is more than a mere delinquenta. MI sees him as a trove of appartunities. It wants to acquire Eyukkmun and put him in a bunker lab far from public eyes. I could nat get many details about how they plan to nail Eyukkmun, but it appears from the micro-bug recordings that Eyukkmun has already been located and identified. How and when Eyukkmun will be brought in will be discussed in the next meeting."

Nethrapal ended his monologue and stared excitedly at Waghmare. Waghmare was roused by the peculiar story, but still looked confused.

"You have made interesting findings and this would make for a great scoop. But I still wonder what you want from me. I used to have good contacts in media which I still can use in case you want to auction your story to the highest bidder. But then, you have to show them concrete evidence," Waghmare said.

"Saar this was nat expected from a genius like you," Nethrapal said, quite dramatically. "We have a landmine with us and you want to trade it for crackers? Why saar, when we can have a blast?"

"We can have a blast?" Waghmare asked incredulously.

"The way I see it saar, the City is going through a rough period. Ecanamists are calling it recession. Basically ecanamic activity is nat good and businessmen are nat making money. State assembly is abuzz with apposition criticism of gavernment palicy. But is the gavernment really to blame for this? Eyukkmun is to blame for this. Of course there are other factors also causing the pessimism, buta no one factor has been as much responsible for ecanamic slowdown in the

City as Eyukkmun has. He has created such a panic psyche, people have stopped going out after dark. All retail stores in the City close by 7.00 p.m. Hotels are nat making money. Restoorants are nat making money. Tourism industry has come to a standstill.

"BPO offices are closing shap and shifting to other cities, some even to other countries. You see, they have to remain open in the night and work by New York standard time. Even builders are losing money. Land prices have never depreciated in the City. Till last year, land prices used to double every five months. Now no one wants to buy land in this city. It is an unsafe city. For the first time in decades, this city is seeing more out-migration than in-migration.

"News channels are the only ones making money. Whole country is glued to Eyukkmun stories. Naturally news channels keep replaying the traumatic experiences of Yuckman victims. This further aggravates fear psychosis among City dwellers. They have lost all faith in the legal system. Even though there has nat been any Eyukkmun sighting for weeks, people still fear. Why? Because Eyukkmun has nat been caught. He can come back anytime, anywhere.

"Now consider the situation in which we have Eyukkmun. We can tell the public at large that we have nabbed him. But we can control the *timing* of our expose. The moment it is out in the media that Eyukkmun has been nabbed, the market will echo with optimism. People will regain confidence in the law and order of the City. Share prices of campanies based in the City will jump many fold. Real estate prices will jump in bounds in a single day..."

"You can sell exclusive rights of the expose to a media company. You can fix bets with bookies. There are many ways of making money out of Yuckman," Waghmare said, excited. "You have come to me because you know I have credibility and reputation among businessmen. I know cash-rich investors in stock exchanges and can sell information at a premium. They will then do insider trading and make a quick buck before media release of Yuckman's capture."

"Yes, Saar, yes. Precisely," Nethrapal said, pleased.

"But all this only if we have Yuckman. We do not even know what kind of creature Yuckman is. You are saying military officers are keeping a watch on him. On top of that he himself is dangerous. Don't you think we are making castles in the air?" Waghmare asked.

"I have a plan. MI has already located Eyukkmun. I will find out where he is and how we can slip him out of MI's grip. As about keeping him in control, it is nat going to be a big problem. We will make a container of tempered glass and fill it up with helium or some other inert gas. Inflammable gases coming out of Eyukkmun's body will nat run the risk of burning in an atmosphere of inert gases. Tempered glass will ensure he does not break out of the container. We keep him without shit or other wastes, the biogas plant inside him will nat get its fodder. He will get weaker and weaker. Keeping him in our custody will then become even easier.

"I know thata you had kept many goons in Necrosis payroll. Some of them have earlier been implicated for robbery and bank jobs. You used them for intimidation at the behest of clients. We will need them."

"Do you plan to confront army officers with thieves?" Waghmare said nervously, "This is felony. Also remember that you are dealing with army here, not the lousy police."

"Yes. The rewards are worth the risks. Let me get more details and lay my strategy. I will also need funds to execute the plan," Nethrapal said.

"Money is not a problem. The risks are too high. When we go public with Yuckman, MI will ultimately realise we snatched their hunt. They do not operate like local police or even RAW. They are dangerous and not amenable to influence. Give me some time to think."

"Saar!" Nethrapal said slyly, "You still haven't understood the reason why I have approached you. There are many other lobbyists in town. Why you? Because you are desperate for some action. Because you are desperate to get back your influence. Because your career ended before you could earn enough. You are desperate enough to take the risk involved in this job…"

Sibu was in love.

Sibu missed Malvika. She was lying there besides him, sleeping like a child. Still he missed her. Sibu caressed her intricately carved body and kissed her navel. When Sibu had picked her up at the dance show in Garbage Island, he was basically kidnapping her. He was expecting her to scream and resist the abduction bid but she did not. To Sibu's surprise, she was not appalled by him.

"Wow," Malvika had exclaimed when Sibu removed his brown overcoat and hat to expose his stinky self, "you are so beautiful."

Sibu was puzzled and was sure she was being sarcastic, "I know I am ugly."

"No, you are not. You may be different. But you are not ugly. You are like an artist's rendition of a man deprived and disenfranchised by this cruel world," she had said.

Malvika considered him special, a gift to humanity. Over the weeks that they stayed together, Sibu was surprised by Malvika's indifference to his smell, his pathetic looks, his habits of scavenging and coprophagia. Their lovemaking had been ecstatic and divine. Malvika took in as much as he gave. Coition, anal, oral, plural: they unabashedly explored all games of intimacy and fantasy.

After picking her up at Garbage Island, Sibu had found her a lonely yet cosy farm house in a forested area outside the City. Sibu had locked up the lone caretaker in a dungeon inside the farm so that they had the whole farm to themselves. It was a spacious farm with absolute privacy, being miles away from the nearest habitats.

One day Malvika said that the skin pores on Sibu's skin might be symptomatic of skin cancer (Sibu had no idea what skin cancer was) and needed to be cured. The fact that the pores could emit poisonous gases and acidic liquids did not help. Malvika reasoned that he might risk someone's life by accidentally exposing the person to the gases or liquids emitted from these pores. Sibu tried to convince her that he could control the movement of his skin pores. Emitting gases from his skin was just like excreting. But she did not have any of it. She decided to go to the City and get some ayurvedic medicines from a trusted doctor.

The moment Malvika said this, Sibu realised she wanted to escape from his captivity. All the sweet words, all the caring gestures had all been pretence. Ali had said so! He had talked to his friend Ali about Malvika. Ali had said beauties do not date beasts. It is unnatural. She would not indulge him unless she had a motive behind it. Sibu had not agreed with Ali. He had said some basic emotions cannot be faked; they come right from the heart. To make his point clear, he had invited Ali to the farmhouse to meet Malvika. Ali found her pleasing and benevolent. Still he insisted she carried ulterior motives.

"I know the ways of the world, friend. You have come from an innocent jungle village, so it is easy for you to trust people. There are rules governing interactions between people. It's give and take in a relationship. You abducted her. She does not mind, surprisingly! She is giving you so much love and care. What does she get from you?" Ali had asked.

"I love her back. We both love each other. We do not need anything else," Sibu had said.

But Ali was so right. Malvika was just waiting for an opportunity to leave. The boy was much smarter than him.

But Sibu was already in love with her. So intensely in love, he did not have the heart to force her to stay. He decided to let her go. Malvika woke up one morning, casually said she would be going to the doctor and left. She did not even give a farewell kiss. Or even a hug. She simply left. Sibu had meant nothing to her. Sibu cried his heart out after she left. His heart was in pain. He was in pain. He grew violent and started throwing things around. He broke whatever he could reach and ransacked the entire place in hours.

Sibu realised that Malvika must have informed the police and the police would be on its way. It was risky for him to stay in the farmhouse. But then, he did not care anymore. *Let the police come. Let them take me away and put me under the noose.* He lay in a dark corner of the cottage and kept crying.

At long last the door opened and Sibu heard cautious footsteps. It appeared to Sibu that the police had finally arrived. Just then he heard a female voice calling him out.

"Sibu! Sibu baby, where are you?" It was Malvika! Sibu jumped out from his corner and ran across to the living room like a little kid running to its mother after a bad dream. Sibu hugged her as if he would never again get a chance to, and cried.

"Sibu! What has happened here? Why is everything in a mess?" Malvika asked even as he sobbed on her shoulder. "You are like a child. I leave you for, what, half-a-day and you make a mess of the whole place?"

"I thought you would never come back," Sibu said.

"Oh my baby, who gave you such an idea? I had gone to the City to get you some medicines," Malvika said.

"Ali said," Sibu explained between his tears, "he said it is not natural for a beauty to *like* a beast like me. You were playing a game to get out of my captivity. I had kidnapped you, no?"

"Ali, that kid of what...fifteen or sixteen years of age? Suits you for taking advice from a child!"

Malvika looked at Sibu curiously. "Probably he was correct. I do not *like* you."

Sibu missed a heartbeat on hearing this. Malvika made Sibu sit on a sofa and sat on his thigh. She caressed his face and said, "I *love* you, my beast. I cannot blame Ali. Most people in this dirty world would not see the beauty in you. They are conformists; they have ideal bases of what is beautiful and what is ugly. They do not appreciate any deviation from their norms of beauty. Besides, I have never been loved so deliriously in my life. I have never felt this special in any of my previous relationships."

"Tell me about your previous relationships," Sibu said.

"No, I won't bore you with those…"

"Please please. Tell me about your past relationships," Sibu importuned the way kids demand new toys from parents.

"Well, I come from a poor family. I do not remember my family well. My earliest recollection is that of my mother telling me: being beautiful is a curse if you are born in a poor family. You shall always lead a life of bondage. She left me at a godman's ashram when I was eleven or twelve. The guru used to rape me. He actually had hordes of girls of various ages serving as *dasinis* – holy servants – in the ashram. The guru, although a pervert, took good care of us. We were properly fed. A teacher used to come to educate us. We had a TV room where we used to watch movies too.

"I was fascinated by movies at an early age. I wanted to become a dancer, but there was no avenue to learn dancing in the ashram. I and my friends at the ashram used to dance in our mess, mimicking steps of Madhuri Dixit and Sridevi. I was once caught. Sevaks of the ashram dragged me by my hair to lord Shiva's prayer room and beat me. When they were done, I was made to take an oath by Shiva that I would not resort to such unholy acts in the ashram precincts. Funny thing is Shiva is the lord of dance. As per the Puranas, the concept of dance came to mankind from the Shiva-Parvati dance.

"In spite of the restrictions and strict vigil, I was determined to make a life outside the ashram. I got my opportunity when a foreigner came visiting. Foreigners flocked to the ashram in search of salvation and eastern spirituality. There were far less worries in their life, yet they seemed to be overly burdened with life. Somehow they found our ashram soothing. So this foreigner had come with a big donation. The guru was pleased. He sent a few dasinis to the foreigner's quarters. I was one of them. The foreigner looked funny dressed in a saffron vest and lungi. He had put on a large vermillion mark on his forehead and had grown a fishtail braid. Perhaps he thought dressing like a Vaishnav ascetic would help him experience spiritualism.

"He seemed to be bored by us underage girls...did not seem to be in a mood to have sex. He asked if any one of us could dance. I jumped at the opportunity, not because I wanted to entertain him, but because I wanted to dance. He liked my dance. He visited the ashram frequently and always asked for my company. He was fond of me. I understood the foreigner was my only chance to get out of the ashram. One day, while he was panting after fucking me, I cajoled him to take me along with him. I was not sure if the guru would break ashram rules and let a dasini leave. But he did. He could not afford to say no to a rich donor.

"I stayed with the foreigner for a few months in his estate in Goa. I realised how big a prick he was only after I left the ashram. He was abusive and the time I spent with him was horrible. Now that I think about it, days I lived with him gave me the drive to leave him and go to Cochin. There I tried my luck in the Malayalam film industry. I was told that it was easiest to get a break at the Malayalam film industry. But I was not so lucky. A small role here, a bystander there, a skin-displaying masseur to the villain – these are the odd roles I could manage without a godfather.

"Then I met a local mafia boss. Driven to the edge, I was ready to stay with him in exchange for his financial support.

After some cajoling, he agreed to finance a movie to launch me. However, he placed a condition – if he could not recover his money from the movie, he would recover it from me. I was desperate for a break. I agreed.

"The movie we made was a low budget semi-porn movie. I am still ashamed of it. But then I was desperate for a break. So this was it. The movie never made it to the big screen. It was sold in CDs at many places. But that would not recover the mafia boss's money. Now he got down to balancing his accounts. He sold me to the highest bidder he got – a jobber for dance troupes. I live with this jobber... I mean used to stay before you rescued me. The bastard used to charge a heavy interest on the amount he paid for me. He had promised to free me once I repaid his money along with interest from my shows. But, surprisingly, the sum I owed to him kept increasing. That bastard."

That explained it all. After all that she had gone through, Sibu realised, he had rescued her by abducting her. Her story was no different from his story. Both had suffered. She understood him. She empathised with his state. Her love for him was genuine. Knowing this he loved her even more.

Sibu felt content with her. He was content for the first time in his life. He had no worries, no cravings; no need for possession. Her company was all that mattered now. This very moment, at which he was sleeping with her, was the moment of crescendo of his life. Sibu marveled at how other-worldly love is. Love is the ultimate achievement of man. Man takes birth, lives, and then dies. The value of a life is next to null. The only way it acquires meaning is by experiences. What better way is there to achieve the pinnacle of experiences than love? Sex, wealth, spiritualism, devotion, shit, marijuana, alcohol all are passé. They only give momentary satisfaction. Love opens you to self-actualisation. You find yourself at the centre of the cosmos, oblivious of the traps of mundane life around you.

A hand caressed Sibu's cheek and jerked him out of his reverie. Malvika had woken up. "What are you thinking baby?" she asked.

"About you," Sibu said and kissed her passionately, "about me, about us."

Malvika kissed him all over his face while she climbed over and tightly squeezed his torso with her naked legs. She sucked at Sibu's thick lips as a thirsty Bedouin would suck at a last drops of water in her water bottle in the middle of the desert. Sibu's hands involuntarily grabbed her cherry bosoms and suckled on their warmth. Junior Sibu turned hard and brushed against the wet lips of Malvika's canal in anticipation of what lay within. It was about to pierce in when Malvika let go of her tight grip. She wrestled out of his embrace and looked at him intently.

"You haven't taken your medicines, have you?" Malvika asked.

Sibu was exasperated. The problem with Malvika, as Sibu had found out over the weeks, was that she was obsessively caring. The tablets she had got from a City-based ayurvedic doctor were indeed effective. Sibu had to take a bunch of tablets of different colours three times a day. The gaseous and acidic secretions from his body reduced drastically within days after he started taking the tablets. By now the gases and acidic liquids had completely gone. However the tablets seemed to be having negative side-effects on Sibu. Ever since he started taking the pills, he had lost appetite for shit and industrial effluents. Whereas earlier he could go on and on for days grazing through wastes, now he actually felt aversion towards many delicacies found in gutters. Sibu also felt weak and effete.

Sibu wanted to discontinue the medicines. He had told this to Malvika many times. But she insisted that the medicines would cure him and make him more human... what he wanted. That way his lethal lineaments could be controlled and he would be more acceptable in human society. She was so loving and caring, Sibu could not say no. Then another problem appeared. Sibu, who used to be a lion in bed, experienced problems in arousing Junior Sibu up. This made him even more insecure with Malvika. He feared that he was turning impotent. So he stopped taking the medicines. Malvika would make him take the tablets; he would then choke the tablets in his throat and later vomit them out into the sink.

"So?" Malvika enquired. She seemed to be pissed.

"Whatever gave you such ideas?" said Sibu nervously, "You know I take the medicines regularly. You make sure I take the medicines regularly."

"Sibu, I am just trying to help you. The ayurvedic doctor had warned me of the side effects; but these are temporary ones. Once you are cured, you will feel strong again. You and I, we can go back to society and blend in," Malvika said.

"You had said I am special. This evil society and its people cannot see my beauty, but that does not mean I have to change. Now you want to change me!" Sibu spoke out accusatorily.

"Alright, do what you want to do," Malvika pouted and got up from bed. She wrapped a gown around her and went away. Sibu got up to cajole her. He found her crying in the kitchen. Sibu went to her and wiped her tears.

"You know it pains me when you are sad," Sibu told her.

"I am sad because I am doing something for *us* and you just don't care. All you men are the same. Insensitive and shallow," Malvika said and turned her back to Sibu.

Sibu affectionately scratched at her back and said, "Malvika, sorry if I hurt you. But these medicines are becoming unbearable. Please."

Malvika turned and said, "I wanted to say this at a better time. But if you insist, I missed my last two periods."

Sibu looked on blankly.

"God, you don't even understand that. I am pregnant. Pregnant with your baby. I had brought a pregnancy test kit from the City. I have tested many times over. I am pregnant," Malvika explained.

"You are!" Sibu exclaimed and hugged her happily, "Why didn't you tell me?"

"Because you are still a baby," Malvika said, still looking irritated. "Do you know how big a responsibility this is? Given your condition, I know there will be many complications with the birth. I don't even know how the baby will turn out to be. We will need intense medical care for the baby... if she, or he, has any chance of survival. And what if she survives? What future can we give her? What education, what socialisation can we impart here inside the forest? You have been declared a felon. The police has not yet identified you, so this is our only chance to go back and blend in.

"But then, *you* don't want to change. *You* want to be the way *you* are. It has always been about *you*. I am just a servant girl here to entertain *you*, am I not? Take it from me; I cannot always revolve around your world. I will take care of the child all alone, if needed. All I fear is she does not end up in an ashram like me..."

Malvika started crying inconsolably. Sibu was distressed; he always did something foolish like this, only to regret later.

"Malvika... babydoll, I am sorry. I did not know. Please, please stop crying. I cannot see you cry like this. We will give our baby the best education possible. I will do whatever you want me to do. Please, you know I am just a simpleton. I take time to understand things... " Sibu pleaded.

Men of filth

There were three great personalities of the 19th century whose ideas were so strong that they have influenced generations since their inception, and keep doing so. They are Darwin, Marx and Freud. Of these, Freud and his ideas have largely been discredited, especially by the very branch of study he is credited for founding: psychoanalysis. Marx has been proved wrong, time and again, by communist experiments in various countries. Among the three intellectual giants, Darwin still stands tall. For his 'theory of natural selection' is not a theory.

Evolution by natural selection is a fact, a phenomenon. All living beings, howsoever complex or simple, have come to live by mere error. There is neither intention nor foresight in the design of any specie. They are all here by errors in gene structure during conception. Variations that are adaptive to the environment have survived and prospered; others which are maladaptive have perished. This is how a hierarchy of complex flora and fauna has evolved from single-celled organisms.

In spite of the large body of evidence supporting the phenomena of evolution by natural selection, there is a school of thought – creationism – which vehemently opposes the idea of evolution. Creationists broadly believe that the world of living beings is too complex to have evolved by trial and error. There is an intelligent design involved, i.e. a divine being created all living creatures. Their main criticism of evolution is that scientists have not been able to show evolution happening. Evolution is a slow process and happens in a matter of hundreds, or thousands, of years. The evidence of evolution is gathered from indirect evidence, such as genealogy of fossils and evidence from selective breeding. The dog has evolved from the wolf over hundreds of years. What creationists would want, to get satisfaction, is for scientists to show that a wolf would give birth to a dog. And if it ever happens, they would jump onto it and call it a miracle of God.

It is not that instances of evolutionary changes in matter of decades have not been observed. Experiments, stretching over decades, are being conducted to detect and capture evolution. In one such experiment, a group of scientists went to a small islet off the Croatian coast called Kopiste in 1971 and found a species of lizards, *Podarcis Sicula*. It is a common Mediterranean species and mostly eats insects, i.e. is carnivorous. The scientists did not find this lizard in a nearby islet called Mrcaru. They introduced five pairs of lizard *Podarcis Sicula* on the islet Mrcaru. The idea behind this was that lizards on two different islands cannot intermingle; hence separate gene pools develop giving an opportunity for speciation.

Then in 2008 (thirty-six years later), another group of scientists went to islet Mrcaru. They found a flourishing population of lizards. However, the lizards looked very different from *Podarcis Sicula* of islet Kopiste; they had larger heads and bigger guts. They had longer, wider and taller heads which means they had developed a greater bite force. This change had happened because the lizards of islet Mrcaru had, in a bid to adapt, shifted to a largely vegetarian diet.

Unlike in animals, plant cell walls are stiffened by cellulose. Hence herbivorous animals need stronger bite force than carnivores or insectivores. The lizards of islet Mrcaru had evolved heads with stronger bite force which helped them chew vegetarian diet and better adapt to the surroundings in islet Mrcaru. Another interesting development was that the guts in the lizards of islet Mrcaru had started evolving like that of the herbivores. Animal guts generally are not equipped to digest cellulose without the aid of bacteria; hence gut of most herbivorous species has a chamber housing such bacteria (called caecum) and acts as a fermentation chamber. Owing to this, the guts of herbivorous animals are significantly larger than the guts of carnivorous animals. The species *Podarcis Sicula* normally does not have caecum in its guts. But the lizards of islet Mrcaru, on their road to evolution into herbivory, had developed caecal valves. All this happened in a span of thirty-six years between 1971 and 2008.

Something very similar has happened to Yuckman, although the changes in him cannot be categorised as evolution. The changes in Yuckman are intra-generational. Humans do not have caecum; the appendix in us humans is a vestige of caecum of our more vegetarian ancestors. My guess is, when he mutated, the appendix in Yuckman probably also mutated and started functioning as a chamber to hold fermenting bacteria. Yuckman is on a tremendous diet, neither herbivorous nor carnivorous, but of waste. In order to suitably digest and extract energy from such a diet, he needs many different bacteria in his caecum performing different functions.

I have retired, both from active teaching and research. Yet these days I dig up interesting experiments and latest findings for I am in the thick of things as far as the Yuckman investigation is concerned. I was initially admitted as a mere citizen observer in the bureaucrat-military-scientist steered nodal group formed by, as I am told, one of the top bosses of the country. But now I have become so indispensable to the group, officers drop by every other day at my house. I am expecting Colonel Saket Giri here at my house any moment now.

This is how it all happened: some top bureaucrat at the very top gave a presentation to some top minister at the very top about the opportunities and threats the Filthy Fiend poses. At the end he also presented a detailed break up of projected expenses of the Filthy Fiend Exploration, Neutralization and Divarication Study team (FENDS, official name of the team) in the current fiscal year. Fascinated by the fiend, the minister approved the exaggerated budget in entirety and allocated the said monies from Secret Service Funds (SS funds) of the Ministry. SS funds are not audited and so no one can be held accountable for how they are used.

Bureaucrats assumed charge of the team's finances; scientists and intelligence officers were asked to look after research and operations, respectively. This division of labour worked smoothly for some time, till scientists and spies realised that by exerting control over the team's finances, bureaucrats were effectively controlling all activities of the team. The bureaucrats had devised their own system of expense auditing and others had to refer every major decision to bureaucrats for approval. Also implicit in this narration is the idea that perhaps bureaucrats get a greater chance at siphoning away SS funds than the other two camps.

The scientists could not digest this. They reasoned that if the team's core functions are carried out by them and intelligence officers, then why should bureaucrats be in control? They teamed up with intelligence officers and planned to get rid of the bureaucrats. Intelligence officers whispered to senior intelligence officers about graft and mismanagement by bureaucrats. Senior intelligence officers (who have access to many ministers) whispered to the ministers. Ministers enquired from the knowledgeable scientists. The scientists gave an objective and value neutral analysis of how the team's operations have been subverted at every step by the bureaucrats.

Most bureaucrats were relocated out of FENDS. The few that remained were retained for paperwork. For some time after this event, scientists and intelligence officers distributed work and SS funds amicably. Scientists got busy building a laboratory to keep and study Yuckman; intelligence officers lodged a big manhunt to find Yuckman.

Intelligence officers deftly picked an intel that Yuckman maintains a nomadic habitat in Garbage Island. They set up a surveillance team and successfully spotted Yuckman within days. They made plans to cop him in. In the meantime, an estranged bureaucrat made a reallocation of SS funds for successive months, awarding the scientists with a major chunk of the pie. When the intelligence camp objected to it, the bureaucrat said that once Yuckman is brought in, intelligence officers wouldn't have any major expenditure. The scientists, on the other hand, would need more funds.

Intelligence camp was panic-stricken. They were not ready to let go of their influence in FENDS. They intentionally delayed their operation to cop Yuckman. The science camp complained to the minister and secretary that the intelligence camp was being inefficient and would need to be reorganised. The minister and secretary pulled up Colonel Saket Giri, the intelligence camp chief, and gave him an ultimatum to apprehend Yuckman and hand him over to the scientists for their experiments.

Hearsay is that Giri could convince the minister that government scientists could not be trusted on their merits. They keep using jargon words and concepts which others do not completely comprehend. How is one to know if they are right? What if they are not competent enough to handle the situation? Best scientists, after all, work for private firms. If left to themselves, government scientists would go awry. Hence the science camp should have a neutral, civilian specialist as observer. His proposal found favour with the minister and I was called in.

My selection was part of Giri's agenda to infiltrate into the scientists' ranks and find mistakes. Of course I did not know this when, in one meeting, I proposed that we need to do a twenty-four-by-seven surveillance on Yuckman in order to understand his behaviour in his natural habitat.

"Now why do you want to do that? Of what possible benefit can it be? The secretary has already given an ultimatum to bring him into the lab," said a scientist participating in the meeting. The scientists were not pleased with my inclusion in FENDS.

"We know nothing about this man. We do not know what kind of diseases he harbours inside him. We do not know what his bodily limits are; what factors in his natural environment matter for his existence. If we bring him in, we will be keeping him in laboratory conditions. We must realise that this man might be in a sensitive state. Drastic mutations like this can be unstable. Yuckman is precious to us because he is one of his type. We cannot risk losing him because of our own mistakes. Look at an analogy: wildlife conservationists trap endangered animals in order to breed them in captivity. They observe and understand the specie's behaviour in wild before taking an animal into captivity. Without that knowledge we cannot bring Yuckman in."

My argument found favouring nods from many members of the intelligence camp. Giri jumped to the occasion and told the members of FENDS that he would send a spy to understand Yuckman's behaviour. Yuckman cannot be brought in for clinical research till then. The intelligence camp's grant of SS funds for subsequent months was restored in the same meeting.

From that day on, Giri and I have been best of friends. Bosom friends. BBF, my granddaughter would say. I get generous portions of SS funds for my research expenses which will never be audited. I get to use MI perks and IB privileges. In return I sermonise intelligence officers with scientific theories and concepts. Now every intelligence officer in FENDS fancies himself a scientist and drops freakish ideas full of biological terminology at the drop of a hat, and especially so when someone from the defence ministry or the department of science and technology comes visiting.

The doorbell rings. From the impatient ring, it's clear to me that Giri has come.

"Brother!" Giri exults when I open the door. He grips my hand and asks me how I am. Then he walks into the house without waiting for an answer. He spreads himself on a sofa and points me to a seat (making me feel like the guest here).

"I got some good news brother, some fucking good news," Giri says pompously. "That fucker Yuckman is shitty sick. Your antibiotics are working. They are working like magic."

"They are?"

"Yes, they are. Yesterday I got a confirmation from my agent; he is weak and can no longer pump out shit or poison gases. Many scientists in FENDS had ridiculed your idea of giving antibiotics as simplistic and childish. Now they are licking their pussy wounds. I have reported the matter to the secretary and he wants me to take overall charge of the laboratory these bastard scientists have built. We take charge, professor; you and fucking I are in charge of FENDS."

After it was decided to put Yuckman under round-the-clock surveillance in his natural environment, Giri and his team faced a problem: Yuckman usually stayed mobile. He was too fast to catch up with. He had already shown an ability to plunge into gutters and vanish through the large and intricate sewage networks of the City. So both static and mobile surveillance were not viable options. The only option was to introduce a participant mole as a companion to keep a watch on him. Now how does one introduce a participant mole into the habitat of a dangerous mutant?

An officer of MI came up with the suggestion that they should send a female agent to act as his companion. His logic was that Yuckman was sex-starved and perhaps lonely owing to his condition. His act of kidnapping women and keeping them for a while showed his need for female companionship. Yet it could not be denied that any agent who chose to play the role would be in constant risk. Not only that it was gross to even think of spending a few minutes with the filthy mutant, the agent may have to risk living with him. Where would one get such an agent?

Giri and his men went through many agent profiles and zeroed in on 'Intelligence Officer 080FE'. A line of communication was set with IO 080FE and she was briefed about the nature of mission. She enthusiastically agreed, or so I am told.

"This woman is a proper kink. Her file says she has a quenchless appetite for sex and loves unconventional sex. She is open to BDSM, cuckoldry, fisting, cuminmouth and a dozen other things I don't understand and...and... and shitinmouth! Whatever that means, I am not making it up. This is mentioned in her classified file," Giri had said excitedly after she had agreed to go on the mission. "This is a female who loves all that we find gross. She will gel with Yuckman like soda gels with alcohol."

"It is difficult for me to understand why anyone would agree to such a mission," I had murmured, more to myself. To which Giri said, "It has something to do with her feminist beliefs. You see, the bureau uses MICE concepts to recruit agents. MICE stands for Money, Ideology, Coercion, and Ego. One of these four factors motivates a potential recruit to step over and become a spy. Spies recruited on the basis of ideology have been found to be the most motivated and fatalistic. Almost all spies who put their life at risk are motivated by some deeply held ideology. This woman is a radical feminist. Her file says that she had first been recruited to penetrate the flesh trafficking network. When I talked to her, I had specifically emphasised on Yuckman's sex offences and his female victims. She promptly agreed to do the job."

"Sir there is a psychiatrist report in the file. It says that she is borderline psychopath and unstable. She is confused and troubled. She relishes in perversion but later feels guilty about it; then projects her guilt on others. This, the report says, is also a way by which she rationalises her nymphomania. The file also cites many instances of insubordination by her, owing to which she is assigned to missions in rarest of rare situations. I think we should explore other options before zeroing in on her," a junior officer observed with a frown.

Giri does not like dissent. He made a mental note to replace the officer who had dared to raise doubts on his choice and then said with a straight face, "Son, if you think your mother can do the job, be my guest. Of course I don't doubt your mother's skills at making love with monsters but I doubt Yuckman would be interested in the old lady. Other than her and zero-eight-zero-F-E, we don't have many women with that kind of kink and hypersexuality. Don't you think so?"

I have met IO 080FE once, just before she started her mission. She is a beautiful girl in her mid thirties. I had piety for her before I met her, but after I met her I realised that she was looking forward to the mission. I saw naked aggression and recklessness in her eyes. She was probably also on drugs. I suggested that whatever she did, she should not let Yuckman have unprotected sex with her. She laughed asking if Yuckman has AIDS. I tried to explain to her that Yuckman was infected by a retrovirus. AIDS is also caused by a retrovirus, but this is an unknown retrovirus and probably spreads by contact of bodily fluids.

But she did not heed to my advice. It was revealed from the intelligence reports she used to send. She had, quite easily, seduced Yuckman and moved in with him to a lonely farmhouse. She regularly indulged in unprotected copulation with him and, from the descriptions in her report, seemed to take delight in it. Nevertheless, her reports were rich in substance and gave deep insight into Yuckman. The reports contained details of Yuckman's family background and past life, the conditions in which he transformed into Yuckman, his powers, his eating habits, and so on.

After getting these details I preferred the idea of bringing Yuckman into the laboratory. But Giri was not willing to; he was busy playing politics. Inside FENDS, I could empathise more with the scientists who were actually interested in research. This was a rare opportunity and any scientist would be willing to explore the mutant, I being no exception. But I was Giri's man. I was in FENDS as Giri's pawn; I had no place in the team, save by Giri's grace.

Giri was trying to secure the post of chief of all research on Yuckman. While he pulled strings in the corridors of power, he asked me for a way to stall Yuckman's arrest. I suggested that we give Yuckman a concoction of some common antibiotics and see its effect on him. There was nothing novel about the idea and followed from the logic that the biogas system inside his body works by anaerobic digestion which needs bacteria. If relevant antibiotics manage to isolate the bacteria, it would render Yuckman weak. Nevertheless, when

I suggested it to a full-team meeting, many scientists objected that it is dangerous to give him any medication without cross-checking his anatomical features. They were right: antibiotics could create complications for his liver and we don't know what critical conditions persisted inside his body. The proposal was rejected.

Giri, not being one to lose a battle, went up to the secretary and convinced him of the need to feed Yuckman on antibiotics for a couple of weeks. If Yuckman was put on antibiotics, the symbiotic bacteria in his body could not effect anaerobic digestion, thereby reducing Yuckman's powers. It would then be easy to bring him into the laboratory. The secretary conferred and IO 080FE started giving antibiotics to Yuckman.

Giri has lost sight of the real purpose of FENDS. It is no longer about Yuckman, or the opportunities that research on him will yield. I have tried to reason with him many times, but to no effect. He is self-opinionated and unyielding.

"Giri saab," I say, "now that Yuckman is sick and our purpose is solved, we should arrest him and bring him into the lab. It's high time we put him under the microscope."

"What's the hurry, professor?"

"The decision to feed antibiotics to Yuckman might turn out to be a wrong decision. You see, what runs inside his body is a complex system and complex systems should not be meddled with if we are not sure how they respond to external factors. The very fact that Yuckman is sick is worrying me. For our sake I hope he is resilient. FENDS is a means to an end. Yuckman is the purpose why FENDS was created. If Yuckman becomes a casualty to bad decisions of FENDS, we may be hurting ourselves."

I am slightly agitated as I explain this.

"Hmm," Giri says and takes out his cell phone, "if that's what you want brother, I shall make preparations to bring him at this very moment."

He dials a number and speaks into the phone, "Lal? Yes Lal. Bloody prepare the hunting team. Our safari will be leaving next Friday... got it? Yes... yes. Righto."

I notice a slight trembling in my pen while Giri is talking on the phone. After he leaves, I take a close look at my pen. It's a black Parker pen, gifted a long time back by a student. This is not the first time that I see it trembling. It may be the first time I mark the trembling, but it definitely is not the first time I have seen it tremble. I feel I have seen the pen shake earlier, although I definitely have been absent-minded about it. Why did the pen shake? What could possibly animate a pen? Am I hallucinating? Or is it just the shakiness of old age? I sigh in resignation and put the pen back into my pocket.

This is a story that had faded in Sibu's memory for a long time now. It came back to him in a flash, while he was ruminating over the past and the present, and the bridges of time connecting the different worlds of past and present. These days he thought a lot. The ayurveda medicines Malvika was administering on him were indeed working. Yet the medicines left him weak and sick. Malvika comforted him saying that the medicines were strong and the sick feeling would go once the complete course of ayurvedic medicines was administered.

These were the days when Sibu simply lay on the bed, exhausted and tired. He got intense urges for shit and sewer juice, but he controlled himself. This was for his child; for the family. The medicines were doing funny things with his stomach. He no longer felt the fire and intensity inside him, that which had supplied vitality and power to his whole body. Still he took his medicines religiously – it was for the child to come.

The story flashed back from the deep, forgotten synapses of his memory while he was lying in bed, weak and impotent. The story was narrated to him, when he was ten, by an old woman of a nearby village. She was rumoured to have visions that always come true. Very many people from very many tribes from far and near visited her and consulted her. But she rarely opened her mouth. When she did, she spoke the truth.

Sibu was not there to visit her. An uncle had taken him on an outing to the old woman's village. Once there, the uncle decided to call on the fortune teller, for he believed she had rightly predicted his son's birth. The uncle reached the fortune teller's hutment with an offering of jackfruit and coconut. The fortune teller, a wizened and heavy creature, looked imposing. She had coins burned down on both sides of her nose. There were multiple piercings on her lips and forehead. Her eyes were bulging and she heaved like a bull. She looked every bit like a human possessed by gods and demons.

The uncle made his offering, touched the old woman's feet and started to leave.

"Stop," the old woman said. It startled both Sibu and his uncle, for she had a reputation for being taciturn, and almost never spoke without being asked about something.

"Come here boy. What is your name?" she asked.

"Sibu," said Sibu.

"Ask your uncle to wait outside the hut. I have a story to tell you," she had said. The uncle immediately obeyed and went out, although Sibu was not so sure he wanted to be alone with the frightening old woman.

Sibu looked at her apprehensively, "I do not like stories" he lied, just to get out of the situation.

"Still you will have to hear this story," she replied in a deep voice. "My stories are stories of the ancestors...these are stories that have been passed on from one generation to another. These stories are all secret stories, for they contain in them wisdom and insight common man should not be privy to. If any story falls onto the ears of a common man, he would colour it with his own menial perceptions. The story will then travel from one person to another, to another, and yet to another, until the story ends up severely mutilated... until there is no more wisdom left in the story. So you hear me child, this is a story meant only for you. Keep this in your heart and derive strength from the story."

The wizened fortune teller paused and wet her lips with her tongue.

"The river Kolab that flows through our valley is a tempestuous river. It derives its power from Kolab Goddess. Kolab is a beautiful girl, a child goddess, known for her magical, soothing voice. Gods and goddesses come from far and wide to listen to her sing. It is said that water that flows from her hands can cure any disease and fertilise any land.

"Kolab was a carefree girl, never quite interested in politics. That is why she seldom participated in meetings and conferences of gods and goddesses. A lesser god told her about the merry making, the fantastic treats and festive dances accompanying such conferences, so she decided to attend one conference. The conference was hosted by Dharama, the mean, calculative bastard. By sheer misfortune, Dharama developed a fancy for her. He tried to make lustful overtures to her. Kolab disapproved of every move Dharama made. Poor girl, she did not know how conniving and evil Dharama was..."

"My mother says Dharama is the God of gods, that he is benevolent and kind," Sibu interrupted.

"Your mother does not know him. Dharama is unscrupulous and wicked. It is by playing dirty tricks he gains powers and calls himself the God of gods," the old woman said. It was clear to Sibu that she had something personal against Dharama.

"I will tell you how low Dharama can stoop," the old woman said. "Kolab was the purest of spirits. She was a child. Dharama, that old wolf, wanted her to succumb to his desires. I cannot explain what this means, you are still not of age to understand. Suffice to say that Dharama wanted to violate the poor girl's modesty.

"Dharama's ego was hurt when Kolab reproached him. But he was not one to take things lying low. He had developed a perverse liking for Kolab, and decided to control her. Dharama, shrewd that he was, had many friends in the plains. He summoned an engineer from the plains and asked him to approach Kolab. The engineer approached Kolab and told her that he could produce electricity from the vast Kolab river if she allowed him to build a dam across the river. Electricity would bring prosperity to the villages. He laced his proposal with sweet and flattering words, and Kolab could not see through his deception.

"Being a do-gooder, Kolab agreed to his proposal. His proposal effectively put chains on the free flow of the Kolab river, thus restricting her and nature. The engineer brought other engineers and workers from the plains and set about building his dam. He had hidden from Kolab the fact that to build the dam he would submerge thousands of villages and vast stretches of forests. This deception became clear to Kolab only after the dam was built. Kolab cried and tears of blood rolled down her eyes. Other gods and goddesses tried to console her. But she was just inconsolable.

"Kolab became distraught and depressed. She remained like this for years. At long last, Jalini – the great goddess of water and mother of Kolab – cajoled her back. When Kolab came back to the valley, she found the second deception of the engineer. The engineer had constructed more dams and more canals and water from her river was diverted to plains beyond the ghats. Kolab realised that she was now under the mercy of the engineer and his men.

"Dharama came by and chided her. He said that the engineers were his men and loyal to his word. He tried to entice her by saying that he would allow Kolab to have her say in running of the river only if she surrendered her modesty to him. Kolab said no to his face. Dharama was infuriated. He threatened her with dire consequences if she did not succumb to his will. Dharama chased her around, across the world from one end to the other, and caused her much mental agony. None of the gods dared to come out in the open to help the poor girl while Dharama tried to molest her.

"What do I say child, these were bad times for the divinity and mortals alike. What values then remain, if a girl is chased around by a thug and no one dares to protect her? But don't you for a moment think that Dharama, that bastard, or his evil engineer friend, could get away with it. It is the rule of nature: you pay for your deeds.

"You answer for every act. There is a Great God who maintains accounts of good and bad deeds of all – mortals and immortals. At the end, all deeds balance out. Excessive cruelty means excessive suffering. Everyone is answerable to the Great God of deeds.

"Dharama had cornered Kolab in a huge concrete building of the engineers, far from any water source. Kolab could not even call her mother, the great goddess of water Jalini, for help. The building was located in a valley called Bariniput, flanked on either side by huge mountains, but far from any water source. Here Dharama savagely pulled at Kolab and tore her dress apart. In a last ditch effort, Kolab cried and pleaded Ghatisaa, the great god of mountains, to help her.

"'Foolish girl, no one can save you from me. Ghatisaa is in sleep. He sleeps for millions of years and wakes up only for a moment or two. He cannot come to your help. Besides, why would he come to your help?'

"To this Kolab replied, 'He will come to my help because he is a Great God. Great Gods are just and fair'.

"'So where is he?' Dharama laughed derisively as he tried to tear her undergarments apart. Just then, the ground shook like it had never shaken before. Earth jolted the way stray dogs shiver in extreme winter. Great God Ghatisaa had woken from his sleep. In the rare occasions that he wakes up from his sleep, Great God Ghatisaa causes monumental destruction. This time most concrete buildings of Bariniput crashed to the ground. The dam developed cracks, through which waters of Kolab river first percolated and then broke through. The dam crashed and the Kolab river again coursed through the valleys that you see it going through.

"In the few moments that he was awake, Great God Ghatisaa snatched much of Dharama's powers. This was not the end of it. Great Goddess Jalini too cursed Dharama and stripped him of many of his other powers. Then other gods and goddesses came forward, emboldened, and revolted against Dharama. Dharama was literally banished from earth for many years. The engineer too got his punishment for dancing to Dharama's tunes.

"Remember this story child, for I see in you gods and demons. There is good and bad in every mortal and why not when gods can be bad too. The lesson is not to let oneself be cruel, for evil deeds always come back to you. I am no fortune teller, child, but I sense things. I cannot see your destiny, it is for you to make. It is for you to decide. Decide it by doing good deeds."

Sibu could not understand why he remembered this story. He was also surprised by how vivid the memory was. He could clearly visualise the old woman narrating the story. Sibu wondered if he had ever done any evil deed. He wondered if the bad deeds done by him were greater in number than the good deeds he had done. And what about evil deeds done to him? And what about the people who did these evil things to him...

Sibu was shaken from his chain of thoughts by a loud whisper. He looked around and saw Ali at the window. With great effort he rose from the bed and dragged himself to the window.

"Hey old friend," Sibu said slowly, "what are you doing at the window? Come inside."

"I cannot come inside. I do not have much time friend. I have come to warn you. That woman with you... she is a bad person," Ali said.

"No...no," Sibu shook his head, "you've misjudged her. She is good, and guess what? She is pregnant! She is pregnant with my child."

"She does not look pregnant to me. Look at what's happened to you, Sibu. You never were this sick. What is she doing to you?"

"You are mistaken, Ali. She has brought a few tablets from an ayurveda doctor from the city. The tablets are working fine. I am recovering. I will become normal again. Can't you see, the pores on my skin are closed. They will soon heal."

"Look Sibu, there is something deeply suspicious about her. Ayurveda doctors do not prescribe tablets. They prescribe ayurvedic medicines – herbs and all that. Can't you smell something fishy?" Ali reasoned. "And why does she want to change you when she finds you so beautiful? Why is she trying to cure you, why not take another man?"

"Because she loves me."

"Love, my foot! She is manipulating you. It is not natural for her to love you. Can you not see through it?"

"You are a kid, Ali. You will not understand what love is. Besides, you have never experienced love. You are an orphan. I can understand the insensitivity in you. I sympathise with you, Ali."

"There is something else I need to tell you Sibu. I have been an orphan for as long as I remember. But I am lucky. I was adopted by a missionary and raised by kind nuns. They fed me and taught me. They showed me the path of righteousness and truth – the path of God," Ali paused and looked at Sibu.

"Umm...I don't get you," Sibu said, "You are from Bangladesh, right?"

"No I am not...see...look..." Ali fumbled, "my name is Anthrus and I am a student in a missionary orphanage. I also work for the church attached to the missionary. A kind priest, Father Sodano, had come visiting our missionary sometime ago. He had come from Rome after he heard about you. You know Rome? Rome...it is a foreign land, far away, in another continent after you cross the seas. Father Sodano had come all the way here to meet you. He is a learned man, and some nuns in my missionary say he communicates with the Lord directly. He believes you are a gift of god to mankind, and it is our duty to help you. Father Sodano prays for you. He sent me to search for you in Garbage Island, and to help you in whatever way we can."

Sibu's eyes narrowed in suspicion. He knew the gods and shamans of his tribe despised Christian missionaries.

"Sibu, I am a friend," Ali said, sensing his discomfort. "And I am here only to help. Father Sodano and his friends are perhaps the only people in this world who wish you well. Otherwise this is a bad world. Father Sodano is now in a church in the city. Why don't you come with me, meet him? I am sure you will find him very amiable."

"You are not a friend. You are *the* friend, my only friend," Sibu said fondly, "but I do not trust Christian missionaries – they are always up to some mischief. And they pray to a dead god who hangs on a pole in a funny way. You are my friend, but don't ask me to make friendship with a Christian priest."

"But it won't harm you to come meet him once, will it?" Ali pleaded.

"Hmm, okay. Let me ask Malvika," Sibu said.

"No, no not her!" Ali recoiled. "She should not know anything about what I told you. Promise me that."

"Fine I will not tell her, but I have promised her that I shall not leave the house without telling her. How can I break that promise?"

Ali beat his palm on his head in frustration. He then took out a ring from his pocket and said, "Okay, I will take you to meet Father Sodano some other time. At least keep this with you. There is a GPS attached to this ring. It will help me track you, in case you are in trouble."

"What jipis?" Sibu asked curiously looking at the ring.

"Not jipis, G-P-S. It means as long as the ring is with you, I can find out where you are. It is an electronic gadget," Ali said.

"Oh you are so smart, Ali. Okay now come inside. I won't leave you until you have lunch..."

"No, I got to go. Just don't tell your woman about what we discussed," Ali said and slipped away.

A chat window propped up on Waghmare's desktop.

Naughty20blonde: *babe u thr?*

Waghmare had been glued to the computer all night waiting for this message. This message was from Nethrapal. Waghmare eagerly typed in:

Cooldude4fun: *Very much darling*

Waghmare knew that he was under surveillance by multiple agencies since the Necrosis scandal. This, he felt, was the safest way to communicate with Nethrapal over their proposed heist.

Naughty20blonde: *we will have da party on Friday*

Cooldude4fun: *Friday? Too soon*

Naughty20blonde: *yes, but no other way. unable to find da spot. but wht I understand frm wht I hear... our Playboy is somewhere near da sanctuary*

Cooldude4fun: *We must take some more time and hear more*

Naughty20blonde: *not possible. the pimps will take him to their city den on Friday. after that it will be impossible to get Playboy*

Cooldude4fun: *I have a bad feeling about it. We r hosting party in hurry*

Naughty20blonde: *everything under control. Playboy ill and weak... so pimps r casual about it. they will take him in a truck to da city. Not much security. there is only one way to enter da city...*

Naughty20blonde: *by a trijunction near Gandhi chowk. the trijunction stays deserted most of da time... It will be da best place to stop the pimps and host our party*

Cooldude4fun: *What about OUR pimps?*

Naughty20blonde: *they hav been briefed. they r confident. Playboy is ill... not much problem handling him. we take him out and move to our den... will take us 45 mins to reach our den*

Naughty20blonde: *first ten minutes r da most difficult bcoz of empty road... so we will change vehicle after 5 kms nd load him unto an ambulance. once we enter city limits, too much traffic and too many roads. No way for them to trace us*

Naughty20blonde: *we will reach den in less than 45 mins as traffic wont bother ambulance*

Cooldude4fun: *whatever the case, there should be no bloodshed. or else the pimps may come after us*

Naughty20blonde: *the chaps you sent are not good enuf. i am trying to control... they need more training*

Cooldude4fun: *don't worry. they r just formality. sleeping gas will do the trick.*

Naughty20blonde: *yes. i hope so. i went thru much trouble to get it.*

Naughty20blonde: *actually there is nothing like sleeping gas. the incapacitating agents they show in movies and write about in pulp fiction are just fiction. knockout gas is fiction. luckily i found from a source about "kolokol-1", an incapacitating agent developed in secrecy by Russian military. it has the same effect that knockout gas has in James Hadley Chase books. it will do the trick for us. it was used against Chechen terrorists in 2002 after they seized a*

	Moscow theatre and held many civilians hostage. kolokol-1 worked. it is also safe... zero casualty
Cooldude4fun:	*good good. did my contact in Russian embassy help you get it?*
Naughty20blonde:	*he has assured me delivery by tomorrow. he seems reliable*

The mutant Yuckman was ill and weak. MI was casual about it. The kidnap attempt seemed to be much simpler than the original plan. It was as if there was some divine intervention to help him execute the plan. Waghmare could almost hear his heart beat hard. A lot was at stake here, and if things went as per plan, Waghmare could make millions from insider trading and culminate it with the biggest media scoop of the year.

The Legend of Yuckman

Friday.

Sibu woke up in the morning and wondered which day it was. Sibu had lost track of time ever since he committed himself to Malvika's ayurveda medication. He felt generally weak and lazy. Lying in bed was all he did – day in and day out. For a few days he managed to pass time reminiscing. But his thoughts were limited. His memories and his experiences were limited. Soon he felt frustrated (and a little embarrassed) of his limited world view and confined experiences.

Sibu wanted to travel the world. He frequently fascinated about going to different countries with Malvika in tow, meeting new peoples and seeing new places. Invariably, his mind would drift towards faeces and crap in foreign shores. His mouth would water at the thought of tasty shits from anuses of exotic foreigners. Sibu was also finding it increasingly difficult to resist his cravings for gutter-food. He fondly remembered the times when he could graze through an entire street's garbage in a single day. Those were the good old days. Now, even though he lacked the voracious appetite, his senses yearned to savour the fantastic taste of all those fine raw dishes of shit and effluents.

That morning Sibu woke up plagued with worry and anxiety. Sibu could not understand the reason for such feeling. Lying in a semi-dark room for days together perhaps led to this uneasy feeling, he thought. All the windows in his room were curtained, making the room look depressing and gloomy even in daytime. Malvika had warned that the windows would attract people towards the farmhouse. Sibu fumbled for the light switch on the wall and realised that it was on other side of the room. He was feeling too the tired to rise from bed; so he called out for Malvika.

There was no response. Sibu called her name louder. This time he saw a silhouette appear at the door. It was a petite girl in high heels, a mini-skirt and a bra. For a moment Sibu was dumbfound. Then he realised he was looking at Malvika. Malvika walked into the room slowly and teasingly, while purring like a cat. When she came close Sibu was happy to see that Malvika was all dressed up: high-heeled leather spikes, a tight leather skirt and a broad, studded belt round her waist, a low-cut blouse from which her breasts spilled out, and a black coloured cat mask. As she approached him, Malvika went on all fours and meowed. A woollen fox tail was hanging from her butt. Sibu laughed seeing it. It looked strangely erotic.

"Meoooow. Yes master. Meooow," Malvika said seductively, jumping on the bed and now moving towards him in a serpentine motion.

"What's in your mind, kitty?" Sibu asked elated.

"Anything you say master! Your pet pussy does anything the master says," Malvika said as she climbed over Sibu's prostrating body. Sibu keenly eyed Malvika's overflowing bosom, his urges for shit already gone. Malvika pulled out a pair of handcuffs from – it appeared – out of nowhere and gently cuffed Sibu's hands to guardrails at the head of the bed. *We are going to do a fantasy role play*, Sibu thought to himself gleefully.

Malvika pulled out Sibu's shorts – the only piece of clothing he was wearing – and teasingly smacked Junior Sibu. She then fastened both his ankles to ropes and tied the other end of the ropes to bedposts.

"Come baby, come," Sibu groaned, "jump over". He flapped out his tongue and licked at her in the air.

But Malvika's expressions suddenly turned cold.

"You horny bastard!" Malvika shouted and jumped out of the bed. She unbuckled her belt and pulled out a short-handled whip with knotted cords and sharp iron spikes embedded on its tail. She lashed the whip at Sibu, aiming for his protruding tongue. The whip slashed a portion of his face and naked body. It burnt through Sibu's body in spite of his thick skin. He scrambled in pain, pulling on his fastened hands and legs.

"Malvika that hurt," he whimpered "let us just start with the sex and end this role play."

"No more sex for you, you misogynist pig," Malvika yelled. "They are coming to take you."

Malvika slowly moved from one end of the bed to the other, coiling the whip around her arm. "Do you know what they are going to do with you?"

"Who are coming to take me? What...what are they going to do with me?" Sibu asked. He was already shit scared of Malvika's theatrics and wanted the role playing to end.

"The officials are coming. They will take you to their lab and experiment on you. They will dissect you like a lab rat and research on the filth that you are made of."

"Okay," Sibu whispered as he lay in cold sweat.

Malvika slowly moved back towards the bedside, raised her arm, and began to lash Sibu's already petrified body violently.

"But that's not fair!" she exclaimed while still whipping him. "You are not a lab rat."

There was a brief pause in which Malvika looked Sibu in the eyes. Sibu's eyes were wide with bewilderment. Malvika, who was seething with rage, suddenly calmed down and a warm expression came to her face. She moved close to him and whispered, "You are not a lab rat."

"Eh?" Sibu muttered in pain.

"You are a gutter rat," she shouted, making Sibu scurry out of the bed, albeit futilely.

"You are a gutter rat, and you deserve to be treated like one. Those scientists value you too much to admit the punishment due to you. The government treats you like a trophy, a pathetic creature like you! You bastard, you have no respect for women. You are a chauvinistic pig. What do you think of yourself? You will go about anywhere and rape any girl you want to? Do you know..."

Malvika had digressed into a long monologue on lab rats and gutter rats and other things that Sibu could not completely understand. He was confused. What had happened to Malvika? Had some bad spirit possessed her? To make things worse, Malvika kept whipping him violently even while talking to some imaginary rats. The iron nails on the whip tail had begun tearing through his thick skin. He shrieked in pain but Malvika was oblivious to it. She continued with her fulmination.

"...and she was only sixteen. Only sixteen, you pervert. You raped her multiple times and then destroyed her face with acid. She was not the only girl you have humiliated. You, and other men like you, humiliate a whole gender. Your mother should have killed you when you were in her womb. Monsters like you should be..."

Sibu gritted his teeth deliriously at the rising pain even while jet black tears flowed down his eyes. He tried to concentrate on what Malvika was saying, for it seemed to him that she was perhaps explaining her weird behaviour. But the pain was overwhelming and his mind could not process any of Malvika's verbal onslaughts. A fresh bout of shock waves passed through his body as the whip landed squarely across his genitals. He flinched in pain and this expression did not escape Malvika's eyes. Her lashes were now directed more and more on his genitals, which worsened the pain.

"...I am sure you enjoyed humiliating those hapless girls. I am sure you enjoyed violating them. Control is so satisfying, isn't it? Disgracing and offending a hapless is so satiating! You sadistic bastard, you enjoyed enough at the cost of the weak. Now it is your time. I am not going to hand you over to the government before you yield to the retribution of your crimes. I am going to..." her diatribe continued, now even more hysterically.

After a few more lashes, Sibu felt one of his balls rupture. It felt worse than death. The pain was more inside his head, as the neurons in his brain went through a meltdown. Malvika stopped her talk mid-way on seeing the ball rupture and speechlessly stared at the damage. Even Malvika was shocked by this cruel consequence of her violence, Sibu thought.

But he was wrong. Malvika threw the whip aside and grabbed Sibu's other ball in her hand. She then gave a mischievous smile to Sibu, which Sibu understood meant only one thing. He frantically pleaded, but his pleads fell on deaf ears. Malvika pulled at the un-damaged ball with the force of her weight. Sibu's screams had now turned into the holler of an animal facing a slow death. Streams of thick, yellow-coloured liquid were now running out of Sibu's genitals. If Malvika wondered whether this liquid was Sibu's blood, it did not appear in her expression. She looked like a woman on a mission. With a straight face she pulled out a short knife from between her thighs and looked at Junior Sibu intently.

Sibu could understand, yet again with extreme horror, her next move.

"No. No. Not my penis. Please. Spare me. Have mercy on me," he cried.

Malvika grimaced and said in a mocking tone, "And what do you know of mercy, Sibu? You did not show any mercy to any of the girls you killed."

Now Sibu understood that Malvika was indeed talking to him and not the imaginary rats. And that she was taking some sort of revenge for the girls he had hurt.

Sibu wanted to tell her that he had been foolish to have caused all the hooliganism and deaths; that he was not able to handle the powers he had suddenly found himself in possession of; that he had repented in hindsight. But his mouth had gone dry and his lips were quivering. He could not find a voice to speak. Malvika took poor Junior Sibu in one hand and aimed for its root with the knife in her other hand. She dismembered Junior Sibu from Sibu in one neat move.

Sibu could not feel the pain of Junior Sibu's execution. His genitals had already gone numb. The very sight of Junior Sibu's beheading overwhelmed him. Sibu had a close relation with his member that he thought was special and perhaps no other man possessed. Junior Sibu had been by his side ever since he was old enough to understand what Junior Sibu was capable of. Sibu had a difficult, deprived childhood. Onanism was Sibu's only source of joy then. He would slip away from the depressing temporary hamlets his family inhabited out into the woods, find a cosy place to lie down, and masturbate for hours together looking at the clear sky. After years of practice on Junior Sibu, he had identified and codified twelve constellations in the night sky. Each he identified by the pose of naked girl the stars of the constellation outlined.

Later when he was a wretched immigrant in the City, he missed the clear sky. He missed the fantasy nudes as sighting a constellation in City sky was a rarity. Junior Sibu was with him all along, dangling in front of his emaciated body. His stomach had pained when he went hungry. His arms and legs had hurt from heavy manual labour. But Junior Sibu had never been an impediment. Rather in City winters, masturbating had helped him survive many cold nights. Junior played almost an animate role in his life, at times swinging around carefree, in other times erect in hungry attention, and in orgasmic moments ejecting like a hot volcanic mountain.

And now Junior was gone. Just like that. His friend of good and bad weather, his companion in perversion and preservation, was gone. It felt as if Sibu's soul was cut through into two. How could Malvika cut it off from his life? What right did she have... Is this real? For a moment all this appeared so very surreal to him. How could his Malvika do this to him? Then he realised he no longer felt the pain. He tried to lift his hands. He could not. He tried to move his legs. He could not. He could not feel any part of his body. The general numbness in his brain was confusing. He wondered if he had hands and legs. He wondered if he was human at all; if he ever was a human.

Malvika resumed her whipping after cutting off Sibu's member. She stopped only when she realised Sibu had passed out.

When Sibu regained consciousness, his first sensation was the searing burning and pain in his groins. Reflexively, he tried to wince out of the bed, only to realise that his hands and legs were fastened to the bed. Realisation of what had happened before he had fainted dawned on him. After seconds of adapting to the pain, he realised that two men were staring at him from above. He looked at them and froze. They were tall men with broad shoulders, wearing green battle fatigues. But what frightened Sibu most was that they were wearing frightening masks. Each was wearing a brown full-face mask. There were two large eye-windows in the mask and a small oval, black object where the nose is supposed to be. The mask's mouth was big and vile; it was of steel. A black hose protruded out of it and connected to what seemed like a cylinder fitted to a vest on the man's right shoulder.

Sibu panicked, unable to imagine what rituals these men were about to perform. He had by now realised that Malvika was a witch and that her act of castrating him was a ritual procedure in the sacrifice she deemed to make to whatever God she held allegiance to. But this...this looked horrible. What God is pleased by such painful rites?

Sibu tried to raise his palms in obeisance to the masked priests and cried.

"What is it trying to do?" asked one of them. His voice was muffled due to the mask.

"I don't know. Hmm... it is perhaps pleading to us," replied the other.

"Why is it crying?"

"What sort of question is this? Can't you see its dick is cut off? It is fucking wounded."

"And is that liquid, its tears?"

"It's coming out of the creature's eyes. Must be."

"Why is it black in colour?"

"How do I know? I am also seeing Yuckman for the first time."

"Is it Yuckman?"

"That's what the agent says."

"No. I meant now that it does not have a dick, is it technically right to call it Yuckman?"

The masks looked at each other and giggled. Sibu was moaning, but they seemed indifferent to Sibu's moans.

"It looks so different from the one we saw in the CCTV footings," one of them sighed.

"Yes, but it is the same creature. Look at its skin. Thick skin like elephants. There are pores all over the body. It uses its pores to excrete stuff," the other said pointing at Sibu's bare body. "Look at the torso. It is voluminous. Yuckman has such a huge torso in order to process large amount of refuse and effluents. As per one estimate, this creature can graze away garbage and shit from fifty households collected over a week's time in a single session."

"Wow!"

"Yes. This is a living, walking, talking garbage disposal machine."

Sibu moaned louder, intending to attract the uniforms' attention towards his painful situation. They seemed to be engrossed with their little chat.

"Yet it looks so human. It even fucks like humans, right? The colonel was saying Agent 080FE sleeps with it."

"The colonel is an ass. There were murmurs among the officers when he selected this lady agent. He listened to no one. Now see, Yuckman is badly mutilated."

"Whatever. Agent 080FE fucked it left and right. The very thought of such sex arouses me. I find her damn interesting."

"She cut off its dick and destroyed its balls. Leave that, she fucked this creature and you find her interesting? God knows what perversion, what sickness she is mired with! She definitely needs psychiatric help. And you definitely deserve to get your dick chopped off."

Sibu sensed that these uniformed men were not priests after all, and may or may not mean any harm to him. He pleaded with teary eyes, "Please please help me. Please release me from these knots. I am in extreme pain... unbearable pain."

The masks looked on inattentively. He frantically shook his body on the bed, but the masks seemed indifferent.

"Is it talking to us?" one of the masks asked the other.

"I think so," replied the other, and then raising his voice and waving at Sibu, he said, "Hey Yuckman, how do you do? How do you feel?"

After a moment he asked his accomplice, "Do you think it's okay if I take a snap – say a selfie – with Yuckman?"

"No. It will be unprofessional. Why do you want to take a snap with him?"

"My son is a big fan of Yuckman. I could show the picture to him: that I am chums with the dreaded Yuckman."

"Go ahead, take a picture and put it on Facebook," came a sarcastic reply. Then with a raised voice, "Ass, this is a secret mission. You don't tell your son about it!"

After a pause, the recipient of the rebuke observed, "I get it. My son would anyways be disappointed on seeing such a miserable Yuckman."

The masked strangers were talking when Sibu sensed another man enter the room. "Everything alright here gentlemen?" he asked. The masked strangers just giggled at this. He looked from one to the other in ridicule.

"Why are you two wearing gas masks?"

To which the two replied, one after the other: "Statutory caution, sir. Yuckman is known to emit lethal gases."

"The fire department has come out with a SOP manual about how to deal with a crisis situation when one comes face to face with Yuckman. It positively recommends gas masks. We have spares if you need one, sir."

This new stranger in the room, Sibu marked approvingly, was not wearing the frightening mask. He was dark, lanky and dressed in a striped shirt and formal trousers.

"Fools, you do know Yuckman is on our medication. He is not going to emit any gas. He is as harmless as..." the lanky stranger's voice trailed as he glanced over at Sibu. His face contorted in fear. He moved closer to Sibu, placing a knee on the bed for support. The more he moved closer and the more he saw of Sibu, the more his face was distorted. Finally, he exclaimed with bated breath, "Shit!"

"Shit shit shit!"

The two masked uniforms responded, first one then the other:

"No sir. No shit."

"Even we were confused when we first saw it. There is no shit on Yuckman. But then, it is the real Yuckman. Look at the skin...and the conical nose...also the yellow pupils."

"Stop the bullshit," the lanky stranger rebuked. "I am talking about the wounds on him. He has been mutilated."

"True sir. Isn't it amazing, the way this creature has been tortured."

"And to think a girl did it!"

"This mutant is very important for us. Surely agent 080FE knew it. Our mandate was to deliver him to the lab in one piece. What has, oh God, what has she done! Many heads will roll if we do not set it right. Can't we reattach the mutilated parts with surgery or something?" the man in civilian dress asked.

"Sir, this seems to be a fresh wound. When we entered this room we found Yuckman unconscious. We understood that it has been castrated. We rummaged through the room searching for the... the part mutilated. We did not find it. God knows what she has done with it."

"I think she ate it."

"What? This is preposterous even by your standards."

"Why else would she cut off the creature's... that part? The report on 080FE said she was kinky and liked unconventional sex. Such women love to eat that part."

"Who told you that?"

"I saw it in a porn movie."

"Oh shut up you two," shouted their boss. "Silly talk and hideous masks. You behave like clowns, not soldiers."

The masked strangers fell silent. Their boss was seething with rage. "She will pay for it. I will make her pay for it. And when we go back, she will face the colonel's wrath. That mad bitch!"

He took a deep breath, relaxed and continued, "I had tried to reason with Giri that this spy has an unstable mind. She was attracted towards the mission because of her confused feminist stances. Now look at what she has done.

"The medic who accompanied us is still in the van. I am sending him across. Make sure he bandages him well and minimises the damage. We will start for the lab immediately after that."

"Sir, Colonel Giri is sending more armed men to take Yuckman to the lab. We are supposed to wait till then," one of the masked men said.

"Looking at his condition...do you think we need more men to take him? Look at how he is writhing in pain. We must move Yuckman to the lab immediately and hand him over to the scientists there. I will brief the colonel."

After the dark and lanky soldier left, Sibu heard shouts. Those were definitely Malvika's cries. The officer was perhaps beating her. One of the masked soldiers with Sibu observed that perhaps his boss was spanking agent 080FE. The other wondered why he was not allowed to spank female agents.

Half a dozen other soldiers poured in. They were assigned with different tasks. Few rummaged through Sibu's room systematically. One made notes. They were not wearing masks. Only the two masked soldiers were loafing around. One of them was excitable and cheerful. He insistently pestered others to take a photograph of him and Sibu for his son. His enthusiasm was, however, dampened when one soldier pointed out that with his mask his son would never know that it was him. He was baited for wearing the heavy mask; still he did not take it off citing precaution.

A medic arrived in a while and examined Sibu. He applied external sprays and ointments that gave him a degree of relief. The soldiers unfastened him from the bed and put him on a stretcher. He was taken out to a green army truck.

Yuckman Forever

Giri and his men are going to bring Yuckman into the lab today. They must have reached the farmhouse by now. Giri must be preoccupied with the operational aspects. That is why I am worried when I come out of the bathroom to find fifteen missed calls from Giri. It must be a pressing business concerning Yuckman. I fumble with my mobile keypad and call him back.

"Professor, why the fuck did you not take my calls?" Giri barks irritably from the other end. He is rash but never disrespectful to me. This must be a matter of great angst to him.

"I was having a bath. Why? What happened?"

"That bitch has screwed us, professor. The mad bitch has castigated Yuckman and mauled him over bad. He is severely wounded from her torture."

"Castigated? I don't understand"

"What don't you understand?" Giri shouted in irritation, "A field team has reached the farmhouse and they have found him wounded. She cut off his dick. Even his balls."

"Why?"

"How do I know why? Let them bring her over to my office. I will fuck her brains out. Only then we will know why. My field officers say she admits she did it. Whatever her reasons, she cut off his dick. Now we have a Yuckman who cannot fuck no more."

"Oh, I am sorry."

"Sorry? Yuckman is wounded beyond repair and this is all you got? Fucking sorry? Why are you sorry? Did you cut his dick off? Did you help that cunt cut his dick off?"

"No no. Not at all. I did not know what to say."

"Say what we should do to control the damage. My ass is in the line of fire here, professor. Accidents like this and officers are shunted for life."

I understand that Giri is in distress. He wants to hear some words of consolation. It is a fact that things have been screwed up. It is a fact that Giri is to blame for all this. It is inevitable that Giri will be blamed for the mess and will have to live with shunting posts for the rest of his career. But this is not a time to tell him the truth. I tell him exactly what he wants to hear.

"It is not a big deal, Giri saab. Has she mauled any other part, other than the genitals?"

"No."

"Then it is only the genitals that she has mauled?"

"Precisely professor," Giri barks over the phone receiver, "it is his dick."

"Yes. But tell me, of what use are his genitals to us? It is just the genitals. We want to understand his body's anatomy: the kind of mutation that has happened to him. His genitals, if at all, would have been instrumental in mating him with a female for the purpose of reproduction. But Yuckman cannot reproduce by mating. He is a different species in himself and cannot have offspring with a human female naturally. That's why his genitals are of no experimental value to us."

My parker pen is lying on a table near where I am talking to Giri. I see a consistent trembling. This is not an old age hallucination after all.

"So things are under control after all?" Giri asks after a short pause, more to himself.

"Yes," I say consolingly. "Now Giri saab forget what has happened. Make sure that you take him to the lab safely. It will be fine."

My attention is more focused on the shivering pen than Giri. Giri had it coming. I do not feel any pity for him. I take the pen in my hands after Giri hangs up (which he does after asking a dozen more questions) and look at it closely. I then uncork it to find a transmitter smartly installed inside the barrel shell.

Sibu's mind was clouded. He understood that any chance of freedom stood jeopardised if he did not focus at the moment. He tried to focus, but things were too blurred. He was lying on a stretcher in the spacious back of a covered truck. He was stark naked. A ring on his left hand middle finger was the only object he was wearing. The ring was given by Ali. Although naked, someone had spread out a sheet over him. A dozen men in uniform were sitting inside the truck. They were all heavily armed and sat in a circle surrounding Sibu's stretcher. Sibu could make out the two men in masks sitting in one corner. The men were all chatty. They were talking and laughing. It seemed to Sibu that most of them were talking about him.

Nethrapal was feeling edgy. He was sitting inside a SUV van suitably camouflaged as an ambulance, parked off the road near Gandhi junction. The convoy carrying Yuckman would arrive any moment. He and his team had already rehearsed several times for the confrontation. Two men were put up for surveillance two miles away on the road to the sanctuary area. A large tree had been felled and placed across the road. Most of the goons hired by Waghmare for the heist were hiding behind trees surrounding the felled tree. Each was carrying a heavy canister of knockout (KO) gas and an attached gas gun to spray the gas. The plan was to stop the convoy and then attack the whole convoy with KO gas. All the people in MI convoy would lose their senses within seconds of smelling the gas. Nethrapal hoped *all* would lose their senses and his team would not have to handle anyone physically.

Nethrapal realised that he was sweating. He took out a handkerchief and wiped the sweat from his brow. The team assembled by Waghmare for the heist actually consisted of desperados and small time goons. Nethrapal had expected more from Waghmare. His main concern was that there should not be any bloodshed. It was the Indian Military Intelligence they were going to confront on Indian soil. These goons were taking the heist lightly. He had repeated again and again that they should carry no guns. Still he doubted the gang leader and couple of others had packed guns inside their vests.

"Are you nervous Nethrapalji?" asked the gang leader, who was sitting by the side of the driver. He was a tall bulky fellow. He had multiple scars on his unusually ugly face.

He looked menacing and, Nethrapal suspected, missed no opportunity to deride Nethrapal.

"No. Just sweaty. Increase the AC," Nethrapal said. "Have your men sighted the convoy yet?"

"No. Not yet."

Sibu realised there was no escaping the truck. He was surrounded by heavily armed and strong soldiers. He was weak. He desperately pumped for some lethal gases from his gut, but in vain. His consumption of faeces had fallen to naught since a while. He had lost all his powers. Damn the ayurveda tablets, he said to himself.

Sibu could still not make himself swear at Malvika. She was the most beautiful thing to happen to him. It was clear to him that his present condition was due to her. Still he did not have the heart to curse her. The ayurveda tablets she gave her were probably not ayurveda tablets. Probably she was not even pregnant. Sibu could still not clearly apprehend the motives behind her strange behaviour. Whatever be her compulsions, Sibu was not sure if he should be mad at her.

Sibu admitted to himself that he should have been more careful. That kid Ali was smart. Ali had warned him of the events to come. Ali was probably a genuine well-wisher. Ali had given him the ring that could trace where Sibu was. The ring was on Sibu's finger. Sibu wondered if Ali was tracking his movements. Would he come to his rescue? More importantly, could he trust Ali? By his own admission he was Anthrus, not Ali. Ali had lied to him. Ali wanted him to meet a Christian priest from some foreign land. Why did the priest want to meet him? Why was the priest interested in him? Ali never explained this to him.

Ali was keeping things from him. Like them all, Ali was so complex. All citizens of the City, all denizens of the slums that lay hidden amidst its skyscrapers in abashment, its brazen law enforcement officers: they were all so complex.

I do not know when this happened. I do not know when the transmitter was inserted in my pen and why. I am not anyone important. I cannot understand why anyone would want to snoop into my conversations. The only confidential conversation I have had lately was on Yuckman. My involvement in the whole Yuckman business has been confidential. But if someone really got to know about my involvement in FENDS, he could have easily placed a transmitter in my pen.

I look around apprehensively. If someone has bugged my pen, chances are that my whole house has been bugged. My first instinct is to call Giri and tell him about the breach. He should be cautious in case someone is snooping and has already known our plans. I take a deep breath and try to relax. Then I wonder who could have done this. There is Father Sodano, who had paid an unwelcome visit and tried to influence me.

Then it occurs to me: my house has been under MI security detail ever since I joined FENDS. Giri has made sure that two armed guards keep watch over my house twenty-four-by-seven. There is no chance an outsider could barge into the house in my absence and bug my pen. Giri has bugged my pen. And why would he not? It is natural for an intelligence official not to trust his colleagues. A control freak that he is, Giri definitely must be keeping a watch on activities of all FENDS members. This is how he does it! He has bugged my house to see if I am leaking out information.

He will be glad to find that my loyalty is in the right place.

"An army truck is approaching, Nethrapalji," the gang leader said after talking to a member on the phone.

"Just one truck?" Nethrapal asked, surprised.

"Yes."

"Can we know if Eyukkmun is in this truck?"

"Not definitely. But my men say just one army truck and two jeeps had gone to the sanctuary area in the morning. This must be carrying Yuckman. What do we do?"

Nethrapal received this information with mixed feelings. If they had to deal with a truck instead of a convoy, it is good news. He could lead the attack himself and ensure that there was no MI casualty. It would be easy to spray a single truck with KO gas. A single truck also meant that the jeeps would be trailing behind. It could mean that Yuckman would not be in the truck. Things could go bad.

"Shall we go forward, Nethrapalji?" asked a team member sitting by his side, jolting him out of his thoughts.

"Yes," Nethrapal said, and after a brief pause added, "An element of risk has crept in. But then I guess there is always some risk involved in these things."

The truck slowed down and came to a halt. A soldier sitting near Sibu shouted across the grill at the driver enquiring why the truck stopped. The driver shouted back that a tree had fallen on the road. It would take some time to clear the road block. Another soldier observed it was neither raining nor was there a storm. He wondered why a tree had fallen in the sanguine autumnal weather. A third soldier mocked him for being too anxious. The two weird soldiers in masks were sound asleep in their cozy corner.

Sibu sensed a weak pungent smell. He placed the smell somewhere between shit of a child's gut and a rotten sandwich. Any normal person would miss the smell – the smell was so weak that the source may be described as odourless – but Sibu had developed a heightened sense of smell since his transformation. Sibu looked around and realised that some kind of gas was oozing in from various gaps in the floor and the rear of the truck. The gas was oozing in quite stealthily – in streams of what looked like cigarette smoke to Sibu.

The soldier who was anxious and apprehensive about the fallen tree shouted across at the driver to find if everything was alright. There was no reply. He again shouted. Again there was no reply. Someone said the driver must have got down to help remove the tree from the road. He was not satisfied. He shouted again. Another soldier, a turbaned Sikh, pointed out that three armed soldiers were sitting in the front cabin. They could certainly take care of themselves.

The anxious soldier was still not satisfied. He shouted again. And then he fell. It was so sudden that his mates could not understand what happened for a few seconds. Then one got down on his knees to check what happened. He also dropped unconscious. Few soldiers made noises, but invariably all fell one by one. But the two weird soldiers in masks remained in their senses. They had woken up in the ensuing commotion.

The masked soldiers moved swiftly. They armed themselves and pressed in position on either side of the rear door. The gas had no effect on Sibu's nerves. Yuckman thrived on lethal gases; this gas was harmless.

Sibu tried to sit up, but could not. The damage to his genitals was hurting his kidneys. Sibu understood that this was the miracle intervention Dharama had sent his way. Whatever was happening, it was so surreal that only Dharama could have schemed this. Now it was for him to grab the opportunity. He again tried to rise but his gut pained. His legs were numb.

The rear door opened. The masked soldiers lunged on whoever was trying to get into the truck. Within moments Sibu heard gunshots.

After spraying the truck with KO gas, Nethrapal and one other member of his team went to check the front cabin. All members of his gang were already wearing gas masks. The driver was unconscious. So were three other army guards. Then his men went over to the rear and opened the door. They saw soldiers lying unconscious inside. But they were not prepared for what was to come next. Two soldiers jumped over from the truck and started firing at them. They were wearing gas masks. The soldiers were armed with AK-47s and sprayed bullets at the raiders. This being most unexpected, none of the gangsters standing in front of the guns could dodge. They fell. Then the soldiers took aim at the gangsters carrying KO canisters. KO canisters are heavy. The poor fellows were almost immobile with the canisters fixed to their backs. They fell like sitting ducks.

The handful that remained took cover. The gang leader had fallen. They were all clueless on how to react. One person drew a revolver he had kept hidden. Two others snatched AK-47 rifles from unconscious soldiers in the front cabin. Nethrapal doubted if they knew how to fire an AK-47.

With great effort, Sibu managed to roll over onto his stomach. He laboriously crawled towards the door. He was distracted by the sweet aroma of shit. Someone involved in the gunfight had excreted in fright. But this was no time for such distractions. There would be many more opportunities for grazing through filth if he could escape from the present situation. He crawled through with renewed vigour.

Nethrapal realised there were only four of them including him. Others had either succumbed or were wounded. Goon One was carrying his own revolver. Goon Two was brandishing an AK-47 and seemed to know how to use it. Goon Three was still in his teens. He was fumbling with his AK-47, trying to understand how to fire it. Nethrapal just stood there frozen, clueless what to do next.

Goon One and Goon Two were exchanging fire with the soldiers intermittently. The soldiers had taken cover behind the truck. The goons had taken cover at the front. Goon Three was still trying to figure out how an AK-47 fired.

Sibu resolved that if he could escape this situation, he would go to some place far; a tranquil little world full of waste and refuse and sewer dumps and all the other indulgences mother earth had to offer.

Nethrapal understood that the mission had been botched up. He wanted out. He tried to run towards the area where the SUV was parked. It was a stupid move. One soldier aimed for his legs and shot a round. Nethrapal fell and cried in agony. Goon One and Goon Two fired back at the soldier. The soldier ducked. Goon Three fumbled desperately with the AK-47.

The rifle fired abruptly, making Goon Three jump on his toes. He did not know how to stop the fire. He jumped in fright, repeatedly, while the bullets flew here and there. One or two bullets hit Nethrapal. Nethrapal cursed at Goon Three. Goon Three shouted an apology.

Sibu also resolved that he would not go near any woman anymore. Women were the root of all evil.

But then, he reasoned, he could go meet Malvika. After all, he had to know why she did what she did.

No, not even Malvika. No woman rule.

But what if Malvika came searching for him? Sibu decided that the 'no woman' rule was too harsh. He would decide a case on merits as and when the situation rose.

Sibu was now almost at the door. He assessed his chances of escaping. He could not sneak out as the masked soldiers were standing outside: one on the left, the other on the right. They were firing and ducking. After sometime, one soldier went under the truck's chassis and started crawling towards the front. Sibu understood that he wanted to crawl all the way to the truck-head and take the shooters by surprise. The other soldier was continuously firing.

This was his chance. Sibu dropped down from the truck as quietly as possible and dragged himself towards the forests.

The soldier who had gone under the truck wormed his way across to the front. He shot at the goons from below. Goon One and Goon Two fell. Goon Three dropped his rifle and surrendered. The other soldier then came out. He had already called for help from his cellphone. Backup would be arriving at any moment. Together they took stock of the situation and secured the perimeter. Then they went back to check on Yuckman. They did not find Yuckman.

"Wow!" exclaimed one soldier.

"What wow?" asked the other.

"Yuckman managed to escape even after being so wounded down there."

"He is a survivor. But what's the point?"

"What?"

"Why did he escape? What did he escape to?"

Epilogue

By way of an epilogue, this biographer is tempted to speculate. Hundreds of miles away, in another city, a kid gets a pressing call from nature on his way to school. He rushes off to a nearby bush after his school bus stops and squats over a heap of garbage. He gets immense relief after relieving himself over the heap. And then he feels the mound move. He notices a pair of eyes – frightening, yellow eyeballs – and gets the fright of his life. He shits again, this time out of fear. But the shit does not land on the mound. It is devoured by a mouth wide open, just under his butt. He jumps and runs away, forgetting his shorts.

What finally happened to Sibu is not known. MI launched a massive hunt in the area. They failed to find him. Agent 080FE had left him wounded and handicapped beyond repair. He might have survived to suffer a wretched, deformed life.

Another possibility is that Father Sodano got to him. Sodano's motives are not clear. But then, those who act on faith may profess any irrational motive. If Sodano did manage to find him, I shudder to think what he might be doing with the poor monster in the name of God.

Is it possible that he lives happy and content in an ecospace of garbage dumps somewhere afar? Knowing the diabolical character that he was, it is difficult to believe in a happily ever after.

A note from the author

One problem I faced after writing this book was in placing it in a genre. This is superhero fiction, and clearly falls under the genre of speculative fiction. The genre of speculative fiction in India is still in an infant stage, and I would be more than happy if readers find an "Indian" speculative fiction in the story of Yuckman.

Having said that, this story is also a social satire. The idea of a super-villain novel, firmly enshrined in an Indian context, had come to me back in my graduation days, and I had tortured many of my classmates, over lunch and dinner, with tales of a man who engages in coprophagia and turns into a monster. The social context came to me when I was preparing for the Civil Services Examination conducted by UPSC in New Delhi. I read extensively about displacement, deprivation, and the paradox of development during my preparation. And then I was posted in investigation wing in Bhubaneswar as an assistant director of income tax. I had to travel extensively as an income tax investigator, and got a chance to visit the hinterland of Western Odisha.

I had spent my entire childhood in the picturesque hill station of Jeypore in Koraput district. However, my interaction with locals was minimal and I didn't really appreciate the problems of the local communities in Western Odisha. It was only during my tours and investigations that I interacted with locals and understood their numerous problems.

The case studies on genetics and evolution in this book are true scientific studies. I would recommend an interested reader to go *through Like a Virgin: How Science is Redesigning the Rules of Sex by Aarathi Prasad, The God Delusion and The Selfish Gene* by Richard Dawkins as a starting point to understand the mysteries of genetics and evolution.

A few acknowledgements: at one time, my mother tongue was facing an existential crisis due to the necessity of English as a medium for science education. A group of enthusiastic scientists and engineers wrote popular science in Odia and made it possible for the rural population to appreciate science in the vernacular language. My father, Er. Mayadhar Swain, led the movement, and has been the primary source of inspiration for me.

I am deeply indebted to many friends and professional acquaintances for their feedback and support in making the story possible. My deep gratitude to the officers of Income Tax Department who helped me constructively in the pre-publication phase: Janardhan S, Nilanjan Dey, Waseem Rehman, Praveen Karanth, Neha Thakur, Basavraj Hiremath, Jayanthi Rajan, Ashish Tripathi, Abdul Hakeem, and Nayanjyoti Nath among others. My gratitude to Anjai Lal, Aashutosh Vijayant, Sharat Kumar, Somanchi Sri Abhinav, Kshitij Tyagi, Amit Sahu, Nirmalya Mishra, Tushar Sinha, Shashank Sethi, Sabyasachi Mishra, Dwiti Vikramaditya, Gangadhar Patil, Malvika Nayak, Satyajeet Sahoo, Shubhrashtha Shikha, Chandramohan Thakur, Abhilasha Bharadwaj, Vivek Mishra,

Chandan Nayak, and Sudhir Prabhu. My sincere regards to the team at Srishti Publishers & Distributors for bringing out the book in the present format.